KATA

SON OF RED FANG

KATA
SON OF RED FANG
Wolf Dog of the North

By PATRICIA CECIL

Illustrated by Henry C. Pitz

THE JOHN C. WINSTON COMPANY
Philadelphia · Toronto

This book is dedicated
to
COM

CONTENTS

Chapter 1

THE PRIZE OF THE TRAP

SOMETHING moved in the thicket beyond the logging road. Jack stopped, listened, standing quietly on the mossy ground. All was silent after that first rustling of bushes, but still he waited, for whatever had made the noise in the thicket was sure to move again. Five, ten minutes he stood there, using the woods lore that Black-Crow, the Indian trapper, had taught him.

"To see or learn anything about the Great Woods," Black-Crow had said, "you must learn the first rule of the woods dwellers, which is patience."

In a few more minutes Jack's patience was rewarded, for the bushes crackled again. But still he could see nothing, and he decided to investigate. Soundlessly he moved forward across the moss and pine needles, his moccasined feet avoiding all twigs and dry leaves that might snap underfoot. The Indian had also told Jack he must always be ready for surprises in the woods, and the boy knew the noise in the thicket could be anything. It could be a snowshoe rabbit caught in a snare, or a moose feeding on the spring saplings. It might even be a black bear stuffing itself on pokeberries after a winter's hibernation.

When Jack reached the edge of the thicket, he parted the bushes quietly and stepped into a growth of waist-high junipers. Beyond was a big deadfall, a huge fir tree that had fallen years ago. The hollow where its roots had been was a perfect place for a fox lair or a hiding place for any wounded animal.

The boy listened and watched for a minute more. Then he stepped up on the fallen tree and looked over the other side. He saw a glade surrounded by more fir trees, and in the glade was a snarling young wolf, with one leg caught in a trap.

Quickly Jack remembered that Black-Crow's trap line swung across the logging road somewhere near the glade. "It must be one of the heavy traps that the wolf is caught in," he said to himself. "I'd better go for help."

He remembered then that Black-Crow had gone down the Mamozekel River to Howardstown for his summer supplies and wouldn't be back until that night. Jack sat on the deadfall, wondering what to do.

Suddenly the young wolf lay down on its side. It seemed too exhausted to stand on three legs any longer, though it continued to snarl weakly at the boy.

"That's funny," said Jack. "He looks like a wolf, and yet he doesn't, because his coat is so dark. I think I'll try to get a closer look."

He walked forward, careful not to make any quick movement which might incite the animal to further struggles. It was obvious that the wolf had been in the trap for a long time—its strength was nearly gone.

When Jack got closer, the snarling subsided, and the wolf whined once. Suddenly the boy felt sorry for the wild free spirit held by the chains of a steel trap.

I'd like to set him loose, the boy thought, if I can get near enough. Maybe if I talk to him, he'll understand I'm not his enemy.

"Here, fellow," he said in a low, calm voice. "I'm going to get you out of that trap soon. I don't know how, but we'll think of some way."

Still the animal did not move; he only watched the boy with a steady gaze. Jack tried stretching out his hand, but the young wolf, or whatever it was, instantly sprang the length of the trap chain. If Jack had not been on guard, his hand would have been cruelly slashed by the animal's fangs.

"Well, that isn't going to work, that's for sure," Jack said aloud, still in a soothing voice. "You aren't very friendly, are you, boy?"

There was nothing he could do now but leave the animal where he was until Black-Crow got back, so Jack sat down on the deadfall to study him again. The animal was indeed unlike any wolf the boy had ever seen, for the wolves that came ranging in big packs around his father's dairy farm were huge, slinky, gray beasts. When the stark Canadian winter drove them almost mad from hunger, they swept down to the settlements from the north, to howl at night in a way that sent the blood tingling in Jack's spine. They were always gone with the daylight, safely hidden in the distant hills from the trailing dogs and men.

Those wolves, Jack knew, came only in the winter. This animal could not be one of them, for it was now early spring. Though young, this one was as big as, or even bigger than, the wolves from the north. His eyes, too, were different. Jack had sometimes seen the eyes of the timber wolves as they prowled near the edge of the pastures, glowing yellow and sinister like the hot coals of campfires in the dark. This animal had dark-brown eyes, almost like a dog's, but he was wilder than any dog. His color was different as well, for instead of a wolfish gray, his coat was almost jet-black, except for cream-colored legs and feet and the cream-colored markings around his muzzle.

Oh, well, Jack thought, Black-Crow will know what kind of wolf he is. Then he noticed that the animal was panting. "I'll get you some water, fellow," he said. "Maybe you're hungry, too."

The boy went back to the logging road and walked about a quarter of a mile to a stream running parallel to the road. He found a small hollow log lying on the ground, and after scooping out the decayed part, filled it with clear water and went back to the glade.

Jack waited for a minute to let the wolf see that he meant no harm, and then in an easy motion put the water on the ground and stepped quickly out of the way. The wolf had risen again and stood motionless on his three good legs, growling softly with distrust. Then he stepped forward, still watching Jack steadily, and began to lap the water. He drank slowly at first, and then eagerly, until it was all gone. The wolf licked his chops and sat down.

"Tasted pretty good, didn't it, fellow?" Jack said. "Now maybe you'd like some food."

He pulled out the parcel containing his lunch

and unwrapped the thick meat and cheese sandwich. He opened the bread slices and threw the thick slabs of meat and cheese to the wolf. This time there was no hesitation. The animal caught the food in mid-air and gulped it down.

"Want more?" Jack asked him. "I don't think you'll like the bread, but you can try it anyway."

He threw the bread slices toward the wolf, who again caught the food in mid-air and ate it quickly. After that the animal seemed satisfied and sat down again, this time without growling.

"I'll have to leave now, fellow, and see about getting you out of that trap," Jack said, "but I'll be back. You just wait, boy, and don't be scared."

Jack left the glade and turned back the way he had come, heading in a steady jog trot toward the farm. He had been on the way to get his hunting knife sharpened in Troutville, a small settlement ten miles from the farm. But that errand could wait. As he swung along, he wondered what Black-Crow would say when he heard about the wolf.

I hope Black-Crow won't kill it, he said to himself. Maybe he'll let me have it. I could build a cage and try to tame it.

This was the first time Jack had really thought about keeping the wolf, but as he went along, the idea grew in his mind. The winter school term had just ended, two months early, because an epidemic of chicken pox had flared through the province. His father had given him lessons and extra chores at home, but those did not take up all the day. He would have spare time to take care of a pet.

But a wolf! He wondered, as he approached the farm, how he could persuade his mother and father to let him have a wolf for a pet. He decided not to say anything about it until he had talked to Black-Crow. Maybe Black-Crow could make them give their permission.

Anyway, he didn't even know whether Black-Crow would let him have the wolf. Would the Indian want to kill it for the pelt? Wolf pelts brought a big bounty where Jack lived, high up the Mamozekel River in the New Brunswick Province of Canada. The wolves were a constant menace to the farmers during the winter, killing the stock and occasionally even attacking a lone trapper. Jack knew Black-Crow had no love for them.

At the farm his mother was surprised to see him back so early. "Didn't you get your knife fixed?" she asked. "It certainly should have taken you longer than this to get to Troutville and back."

"No, Mom," said Jack. "I changed my mind. I can go next week. There're some things I forgot to do around here."

Mrs. Miller looked at him sharply, but she was a busy woman and had little time to waste in wondering what her children were doing. They had been raised in the wild backwoods district and had learned early to take care of themselves. As long as they did their chores, she was satisfied.

"All right," she said. "It's your business. You're thirteen and old enough to know what you should do. Remember you must have that knife fixed soon so you can help Dad this summer with tanning the pelts. Don't put it off too long."

"I won't, Mom," Jack said. "I'll do it this week, I promise."

He spent the rest of the day in the lot behind the main barn, collecting spare boards for a cage. He put them all in a pile under an old chicken shed, and by the time he had finished, his mother called him to supper.

At the table Jack fidgeted nervously, wondering when Black-Crow would come. He hardly touched his food, and Suzy, his sister, kept asking him what was wrong. "Why don't you tell me some stories?" she begged.

"I can't tonight, Suzy," answered Jack.

Usually he told the eight-year-old Suzy stories of the things he saw in the woods. This night, especially, he was bursting with his secret about the wolf, but he didn't dare tell anyone in the family yet. He had to talk to Black-Crow first.

Suzy liked to have him tell her about the animals he saw while he was out doing his chores or roaming the upland fields. The settlement was deep in the wilds, and often the animals came onto the farmland itself.

Sometimes early in the morning a buck deer would come into the back pasture, mingling with the cows, to feed on the sweet grass. When the sun came up through the morning mists, Jack often saw the buck disappearing into the dark fir woods like a feathery shadow. Suzy loved to hear about him, and Jack knew how excited she would be about the young wolf, but tonight he had to wait and say nothing.

After supper he slipped out the back door and down to the boat landing on the river that ran across a part of the farm. He sat down on the small dock and put his head back against a post, settling himself to wait for Black-Crow. The Indian would stop at the farm for the night, Jack knew, before heading on upstream to his cabin far up in the rugged wild hills near the headwaters of the Mamozekel.

Jack's thoughts kept turning to the wolf, alone in the glade, tired and with one leg badly hurt. That leg must be getting pretty stiff by this time, Jack thought, but at least he'd had that food, and the water to drink. It won't be long now until Black-Crow and I can get him out.

Then the horrible thought occurred to Jack that maybe Black-Crow wouldn't give him the wolf. Maybe the Indian really would insist on killing him for the pelt, or just because he didn't like wolves in general. An ache started down in the pit of Jack's stomach, remembering the eager way the wolf had gulped down the food and drunk the water.

"I just won't let Black-Crow kill him," Jack muttered. "I'll think of some way to persuade him to give that wolf to me. Maybe I can give him some of my allowance to make up for the money the pelt would bring."

Just then, far down the river, the boy heard the faint slap of a paddle on the water. It was Black-Crow, coming up along the far bank to avoid the rapids opposite the dock. Jack knew he would be there in a few minutes.

The boy strained his eyes against the darkness of the water, trying to make out the outline of the canoe by the faint starlight. Black-Crow had told Jack never to keep his eyes fixed on one spot, in the dark.

"Never strain your eyes to see, when it is dark," the Indian had said. "Always keep shifting your eyes back and forth across the place you are watching, and then any movement will attract your attention."

Jack did just that, and in a minute he could see the big birch-bark canoe swinging in toward the dock, with the Indian kneeling in the stern.

As the canoe drew closer, Jack called out, "Black-Crow! Black-Crow, I've got something to tell you! There's a wolf in one of your traps! We've got to go and get him out, and we . . ."

"Can you not greet your good friend Black-Crow without all of this babbling on, like the brook in the deep forest?" asked the Indian, as he swung easily onto the dock from the canoe.

"I'm sorry, Black-Crow. How are you?" said Jack, his face reddening. He was glad it was dark. "I didn't remember my manners, the way an Indian would."

"It is all right this time, impulsive one," laughed Black-Crow, rumpling the boy's hair. "Now, what is this story that seems so important for you to come all the way to the dock in the night?"

"It's about a wolf, or at least I think he's a wolf," Jack began, and told the Indian all about hearing the noise in the thicket and discovering the young black animal. He described how its eyes had been so steady and unafraid, and how it had seemed so pitiful in the trap. "Black-Crow, I want to try to tame him and have him for a pet," Jack finished. "That is, if you don't want him."

"Have you spoken of this to your family?" asked Black-Crow.

"Not yet, because I was waiting to see you. They'll listen to you, Black-Crow, if you tell them it's all right. Will you help? Please, Black-Crow, I've wanted a pet of my own for so long."

"We will see," said the Indian. "In the morning you and I will go early and look at this young wolf, but for now, I will say nothing. You have my word."

Jack had to be content. He spent a restless night, tossing and turning on his bed. He dreamed of blizzards and of the wild wolf packs that howled in the northland, and of a young black wolf that ran alone in the forest.

Chapter 2

THE ARRIVAL

IN THE MORNING Jack rushed through his chores. Black-Crow told Mrs. Miller he was going to look at a section of his trap line and that Jack could go with him. The Indian was a trusted friend of the Miller family, and Jack's mother made no protest. Right after breakfast the two friends left the house, and in a short while they came to the glade behind the deadfall.

"Look, Black-Crow, there he is!" Jack cried. The wolf had struggled to his feet when he heard them coming through the juniper bushes. Jack thought the animal seemed weaker than on the previous day.

"Yes," said Black-Crow, "just as I thought. He is the wolf dog."

"What do you mean?" cried Jack. "What is a wolf dog?"

The Indian chuckled. "This is the son of Red Fang, the largest timber wolf ever seen in New Brunswick. His mother was a purebred German shepherd dog belonging to Pierre La Touche, a hunter who once lived beyond Troutville. I know of this, for I saw the puppies when they were born, and I remember this one. Pierre planned to keep him, but later when the hunter was lost on the trail in the Far North, the young pup turned wild and was never seen again. Now he has come back here."

"Boy, oh boy!" said Jack. "Then he's not a real wolf! He's part dog! That means he'd be a wonderful pet . . . I heard Dad say once that German shepherds are the most wonderful dogs there are!"

"Yes, young one," said the Indian. "But remember also, this black pup's father is a timber wolf of the Far North, the kind that would rather die than be tamed. This pup may be part dog, but he has in him the spirit of the Great Woods, the spirit of the king of the timber wolves!"

"Oh, Black-Crow," said Jack, "do you think I *can* tame him? Does he have a name?"

"That I do not know," said the Indian. "Pierre went north four months ago, when this wolf dog was but two months old. But I know that even as a puppy he was wise for his age, for he had his father's fierce cunning and his mother's great loyalty to man. He should be that best of combinations: a faithful dog, who also thinks and acts for himself, as the wolf must do. We will call him Kata, which is the Indian word for Wise One."

"That's perfect," said Jack. "Kata he is. But how'll we get him out of the trap?"

"That is easy," said Black-Crow.

The Indian drew out a pair of heavy gloves from a large burlap bag he carried, and put them on. Then he approached the wolf dog slowly, watching him closely. Kata had begun to growl softly, and now he crouched, tense, straining against the trap. Jack saw little clots of blood oozing down the dog's foreleg, mingling with a patch of dried blood on the ground where he had been lying. Again the boy's heart went out to the young animal, so hurt and bewildered, and yet so dangerous, facing the unknown danger of the Indian.

Black-Crow picked up a stick and threw it with a sharp motion into the bushes. The wolf dog turned at the quick movement. In that instant Black-Crow threw the burlap sack over Kata's head. For a few minutes the dog fought furiously, snarling and growling, but soon his struggles subsided as his jaws closed only on the smothering burlap folds.

The Indian wrapped the bundle tightly with thongs, for enough air would seep through the mesh of the burlap for Kata to breathe. Then Black-Crow pried open the trap jaws with a huge rock, gently freeing the wolf dog's torn leg.

"See," said the Indian. "His name is well chosen. Like a true wise one, he knows when to fight and when to bide his time for another chance. Do not be fooled by his calmness, Jack. Remember that when you have him for your own, he is not yet to be trusted. He has been running wild for too many weeks to learn again the ways of man in a short time."

That must mean Black-Crow was going to let him have the wolf dog! Jack was so excited he wanted to shout out loud. Even though the Indian had not definitely agreed, the boy knew he wouldn't otherwise have said anything about having Kata for his own.

They started homeward with the heavy burlap bag swung from a long pole carried between them. Jack could not help shivering with excitement as he walked along. Imagine! A pet of his own, and a real wolf dog! One that was the son of the greatest timber wolf of all!

Jack had often heard of Red Fang, the powerful

and sagacious leader of the pack. Even the cleverest trappers had not been able to snare him, nor had the hardiest hunters been able to track him down. Many times during the winter, Red Fang's giant tracks had been found around the settlement. The tracks were easily recognizable because of their huge size, but only once or twice had any man caught a glimpse of the great wolf himself.

"One of those men," Black-Crow said as they went along the logging road, "was Pierre La Touche. One night when he was camped on a far trail, with only his shepherd dog, Kata's mother, for company, he noticed that she seemed uneasy. Suddenly, without any warning, a great timber wolf appeared like a phantom shadow among the trees, just inside the circle of firelight.

"La Touche recognized Red Fang immediately," the Indian continued, "for no man could mistake that huge size and those glittering yellow eyes. And no other wolf would have the audacity to appear so close to man.

"La Touche insisted that Red Fang must have seen him put his rifle on the other side of the fire, near where the great wolf stood. He must have known the man could not reach it without having almost to touch him.

"For a moment," the Indian went on, "the three of them—wolf, dog, and man—remained motionless in the flickering light. Then the wolf whined low in his throat, and the dog answered his summons. She crept forward to touch noses, and side by side they trotted off into the Great Woods."

"What happened to Pierre?" asked Jack.

"He waited there," said Black-Crow, "beside his fire all through that long night—waiting for the dog to come back to him. It was three days before she crept quietly into the camp. Pierre was wakened from his sleep by the shepherd dog licking his face. There was no sign of Red Fang.

"The hunter was happy, knowing that his dog had remained faithful to him against the lure of the Great Woods, when she could have stayed on as Red Fang's mate. He took her back to his cabin, telling everyone he saw that she was a true sample of her loyal breed.

"But all was not to go well for La Touche's dog, for after her four puppies were born, she sickened and died when the puppies were only a few days old. Pierre raised them on a bottle, for they were all healthy puppies. Three were females and looked just like their mother. The fourth, a male, was the largest and the strongest. He, too, had his mother's black and silver coloring and her steadfast brown eyes. But Pierre saw that this puppy had the great bone and size of the wolf. He had a way of holding his head high and his ears up, unlike any dog. He was bold and spirited. This was the puppy that Pierre decided to keep for himself.

"He gave the other dogs away as pets, but this one," the Indian gestured at the burlap bag, "was with the hunter when he disappeared into the north, to meet death on the trail."

As the Indian finished speaking, they reached the farm, and Mr. Miller came out of the barn just as Jack and Black-Crow entered the front yard.

"Dad! Dad!" cried Jack. "Black-Crow caught a wolf dog in one of his traps, and he says I may have it! May I, Dad? I'll take good care of him and keep him penned up away from the cattle, until I can tame him." In the excitement of getting Kata out of the trap Jack had forgotten his own fears about what his parents would say.

"What is all this, Black-Crow?" Mr. Miller asked.

Black-Crow told Jack's father the whole story. "I think, Mr. Miller, that if the boy keeps the wolf dog in a pen for a few weeks, he may become tame. If that happens he will make a good pet."

"Well, Black-Crow, if you say so, I suppose it will be all right. We'll give him a try, anyway. You know more about animals than all of us together, so I'll take your word. But remember," Mr. Miller turned to Jack, "if this wolf dog causes any trouble, he must be shot. I can't have any more mean animals on the farm. The two dairy bulls are hard enough to handle."

"He won't cause any trouble, Dad," said Jack. "You can count on that. I'll tame him, and you'll see—he'll be a wonderful dog."

Mrs. Miller and Suzy had come out of the house to see what was going on, and they went with Jack and Black-Crow to put Kata in an empty box stall in the barn. The Indian had said a box stall would be better than the cage Jack had been planning to build, because it would be bigger. "It will give the wolf dog more room to move around, and his leg will heal faster because of that."

In the barn, Black-Crow put the heavy burlap bag on the straw-covered floor of the stall. With one quick movement of his hunting knife he cut the thongs on Kata's legs, before he himself slipped outside the stall. The wolf dog lay still for a minute, then dazedly shook himself free of the suffocating folds. When the Indian spoke to him, Kata turned and saw them all watching him. Instinctively he sensed danger and glided quickly into the shelter of a corner, dragging his torn leg. He growled threateningly, and lay half hidden behind a pile of straw.

"Let him alone now," cautioned Black-Crow. "He

Chapter 3

THE EDUCATION OF KATA

As the days went by, Jack got up earlier than usual and dressed quietly so as not to wake the rest of the family. On the way to the barn he collected two eggs from the chicken coops and the jug of milk his father always left in the milk cellar. He then poured the eggs and milk into Kata's pan and carefully stirred the mixture with a wooden spoon.

The wolf dog was always awake when Jack entered the barn, sitting in the far corner of the stall, watching the boy's every move. The first morning he growled and showed his teeth when Jack opened the door a crack to put the food pan in, so the boy backed out and left the wolf dog to eat in solitude.

When Jack went back later, after finishing his chores, the food was still there, untouched. He reached inside the gate for the pan.

"You'll have to learn to eat here, too, Kata, the way you did in the woods," Jack said. "But I guess you will when you get hungry enough."

The wolf dog growled. He did not understand the words, but he did know that the boy stood for danger. In the woods it had been another matter, for there the trap had caught him by surprise. There the boy had seemed harmless enough, had even given him water and food. It was the trap Kata had fought until he almost dropped from exhaustion and pain. But then the boy had come back to the glade with a second man, and Kata had been blinded in suffocating darkness, only to find himself still a prisoner when he was released from the trap. The second time he was confined, there was no trap to tear his leg, but the beloved, familiar woods were gone. Kata was shut up in a small space with four high walls, and the boy was still there. The boy must be to blame then, for it was he who stood between the wolf dog and the broad domain of fir forest and open meadow that was home.

There Kata would return when he could escape from the boy's prison. But now he must use all the cunning he had learned ranging the Great Woods. There he had learned to crouch motionless beside a rabbit warren for his prey; and to stalk the nervous woodchuck with endless care. And in the past few days he had learned a new lesson, the lesson of the trap.

Kata decided not to eat the boy's food, for in some way he felt that it was another kind of trap. He had not entirely forgotten a small log cabin and a man who had once scratched his ears in just the right places and talked in a low, pleasant voice. That man, too, had given him food, and Kata had felt bound to him. But things had changed. The man was no longer with him. These other men had made him a prisoner. He would not take food from this boy.

So for two days Kata drank only water from the trough in the stall. Each morning, before Jack did his chores, he brought milk and eggs, and when the food remained untouched, he took it away again. In the evening he brought a pan of table scraps and meat before he went to help with the milking, and again took it away when the wolf dog did not eat.

Black-Crow had said that Kata must learn to live among men again, that he must learn discipline. Jack knew he must win this first battle. If, when he brought the food, the wolf dog did not eat, he must go without. At the end of the second day, Jack began to wonder if the wolf dog ever would give in. He asked his father what he should do.

"If he gets hungry enough, he'll eat," Mr. Miller replied. "I said you'd have trouble with that animal."

On the third morning, when Jack put the food in the stall as usual, he noticed that Kata did not growl or show his teeth, but still stayed in his corner. When Jack came back after breakfast, he thought the level of milk was a little lower in the pan, though it was hard to be sure.

"Maybe he's getting hungry enough, Dad," the boy reported at dinner. "What about holding out on his dinner tonight and waiting to give him the table scraps tomorrow morning?"

"It may work, son," said Mr. Miller, "and it may help to make him a little more friendly, too, if he's beginning to give in. But you don't want to starve him, so be sure to take him a big meal in the morning."

"I will," Jack said. "If he doesn't eat by tomorrow, he'll starve anyway. What will I do then?"

"Wait till you see what he does tomorrow," Mr. Miller answered. "You're right, you can't let him starve. Neither can we turn him loose. The only answer would be to send him to Howardstown to the zoo, where they can force feed him. Otherwise we'll have to shoot him." Mr. Miller looked grave, and the family finished eating in silence.

The next morning Jack's mother cooked lean beef in a heavy, savory broth for Kata. The food smelled so good that even Jack, despite just having had breakfast, felt hungry when he carried the pan down to the barn. When he looked into the stall he thought he saw Kata's nose lift at the scent.

"Here's breakfast, Kata," Jack told the motionless wolf dog. "I'll leave it here in the stall, but I'll be back in an hour. Eat it, Kata, please! You've just got to!" Then he turned and left the barn.

At first Kata did not move. He heard the footsteps recede into the distance, but he was afraid the boy might still be hiding somewhere nearby. The wonderful smell of rich meat made the wolf dog tremble with hunger, and a low whine escaped him. He made a slight movement, then stopped, remembering who had put it there. Again the dim memory of the man in the log cabin, who had fed him long ago, flitted through the wolf dog's mind. That man had disappeared, leaving Kata lonely and bewildered, to fend for himself in the wilds. No, that must not happen again.

But soon the wolf dog was remembering that the boy always came back after a short time to take the pan of food away. Kata knew he must have this food to live, for just as at that time long ago when he had been left alone in the wilds by a man who would not move or awaken, he now felt weak from many days of desperate hunger.

Kata listened, straining to catch every sound in the barn, but all was quiet. The boy did not appear. Slowly Kata began to inch forward across the straw toward the pan. He was ready to leap back at any noise, but nothing happened. When he reached the pan, he sniffed longingly at the meat, saliva dripping from his muzzle. Still he hesitated, until the tantalizing scent of the food overpowered his suspicion. Suddenly he lowered his head to the pan and buried his muzzle in the meat. Silently and rapidly he swallowed every morsel, licking each speck of gravy from the pan until it shone. Then he walked back to his corner, his stomach stretched tight against his ribs, and curled up with a sigh of content. When the boy came up to the stall a short time later, Kata bared his teeth in a silent snarl. He had eaten, but he was not yet tamed.

Jack stopped short when he saw the empty pan. The wolf dog was still in the corner, just as before, but there was no mistaking it, he had eaten the food! Jack wanted to rush into the stall and put his arms around the wolf dog! Instead, he stood quietly by the gate, knowing that any sudden move would undo all of his work. For now he would have to rely on the food and on his voice, and he would have to get Kata used to the sound of the latter.

"Good boy, Kata," Jack said, trying to keep the excitement out of his tone. "You did eat your breakfast, and you're as smart as Black-Crow said you were!

"And," the boy continued quietly, "maybe you'll feel better now. You see, Kata, I'm not going to hurt you. I'm your friend, and pretty soon you're going to know it."

That night when Jack took out the bowl of scraps his mother saved from dinner, Kata was still in the corner. This time he did not growl. Jack set the pan down, not staying to watch Kata eat. Black-Crow had said to wait until the wolf dog made the first gesture of friendship. Jack was no longer impatient. The first, and hardest, step was over.

After a few days Kata's leg was much better. The constant licking and moving around in the stall had nearly healed it, and the wolf dog was able to walk without limping. Several times when Jack came into the barn he found the wolf dog out of his corner. And one morning when the boy came in with the eggs and milk, Kata was standing in the straw in the middle of the stall. When Jack opened the door to put the pan inside, the wolf dog did not move away. This time Jack waited outside the gate, watching. In a minute Kata deliberately walked forward and began to drink the milk, paying no attention to his visitor.

When the wolf dog had finished, the boy began to talk to him. "Guess you're beginning to get used to me now, fellow. Maybe it won't be too long before we're friends." Kata took no notice of the words, but at least he did not seem frightened.

Several mornings later Jack knew that the battle was half over. Kata had finished the milk, and was curled up in the corner with a contented sigh, his head on his paws. The wolf dog was no longer suspicious, or he wouldn't be going to sleep while someone was still standing by the door! Jack rushed off to do his chores, but he was bursting with the good news. After finishing his work, he ran to tell everyone. Mr. Miller was very pleased, and Suzy begged to be allowed to go inside the barn to look at Kata, but her father said he thought it would be better to wait a little while longer. "Let Kata get used to one person at a time," he said. "He's Jack's pet, and he must learn to know Jack first."

Each time the boy went near the stall he talked to Kata, and soon he began to go into the barn often during the day. He sat on the stall gate, always speaking in a low voice and constantly repeating the wolf dog's name, so that Kata would become used to it. Jack knew Kata had no idea what the words meant, but at least the wolf dog never growled now when he heard Jack's voice.

About three weeks after Kata had come to the farm, Jack found Kata standing at the gate when he went into the barn to feed the dog one morning. Kata backed off when he saw Jack, but he went only as far as the middle of the stall. When the boy put the pan down and went out, Kata came unhesitatingly forward to lap the milk.

Jack sighed. "I wish you were waiting to see me, instead of the milk, Kata. But I guess it's a good sign that you're waiting for food. You know I bring it, don't you, fellow?"

It was true that the wolf dog's suspicions were beginning to fade. Jack's regular appearance with the food had become an established routine in Kata's day. He still felt no friendship for the boy, but he was no longer really afraid of him. Jack kept his distance and did nothing to arouse the wolf dog's fears.

Soon Kata began to look forward to the boy's coming, for it broke the monotony of the days in the stall. There was little to do except sleep, or, as his leg healed, to chase the occasional barn rat that ventured into the straw in search of grain.

When Jack sat on the gate and talked to him, the wolf dog liked the sound of the boy's voice. Somewhere, deep in his mind, still another memory began to stir—a memory of the man who had disappeared. That man had left Kata alone in the Great Woods, it was true, but he had also petted the wolf dog, rubbing his sensitive ears and forehead in a way the young puppy once had loved.

A deep memory, long asleep within his brain, returned now to the wolf dog. A memory of sitting for days in the camp by the northern trail, longing for the sound of a low voice and the touch of a hand that never came. That man, too, had talked to him, just as this boy did, and the wolf dog began to remember how good it had been to sit beside the man, and to have gentle fingers fondle his ears.

Many weeks had passed since that time, and much had happened to bind the wolf dog to the Great Woods. But, in the solitude of the stall, that feeling he had had for the man returned slowly. Now, bit by bit and day after day, as Jack's voice soothed the wolf dog's wild spirit, the yearning for human companionship came back to Kata. He did not know that his mother's blood was also strong, as strong in its own way as that of the wolf pack. Hers was the blood of a breed of dogs that had served man for generations, and it could not be discounted lightly.

So Kata began to move closer to the gate where Jack sat each day. When the boy did not move, but only spoke in a quiet voice, the wolf dog was lulled by the sound and by his own faint stirrings of feeling. When he had run wild in the Great Woods, there had been no chance for those feelings to take root. But here, in the barn of a man, a different atmosphere prevailed, and the wolf dog was responding to it.

One day Jack slid quietly off the gate and stood inside the stall while he talked to Kata. The wolf dog did not move. Jack knew that the first real expression of love must come from the dog, as Black-Crow had directed, but the boy sensed that at least Kata no longer regarded him as an enemy. Jack felt that by going into the stall, on the wolf dog's own ground, it might hasten the taming process.

Finally there came another morning when Jack brought Kata's food and remained standing beside the pan. "I have a feeling the right time has come, Kata," the boy said. "Come on, boy." The wolf dog backed off, but in a minute he came forward and began to lap the milk, with the boy still standing beside the pan!

All the while the wolf dog was eating, Jack continued to talk to him. "Kata," he said. "Good dog, Kata." When the wolf dog finished his meal, he raised his head but did not leave his position. The pan, the milk, the boy's trousers in front of his muzzle—all had a familiar scent, and he felt no fear and almost no distrust.

Somehow he did not want to move away; he wanted to stay there beside the boy, to listen to his soothing voice. Suddenly, Kata wanted to feel the boy's hand on his head. He made no move, however; the weeks in the Great Woods had taught him well the lesson of holding back before the unknown. But the feeling was there, and when the boy left the stall, Kata walked slowly behind him to the gate.

All that day the wolf dog paced around the stall, for Jack did not return, as was his custom. Kata grew more and more restless. He could not know, however, that Jack had noticed his behavior of the morning and wanted to give the wolf dog a chance to miss him.

That night when Jack came with the food, Kata was waiting for him at the gate. Jack gave him the meat, and Kata ate quickly. Then the dog stood motionless, his great, dark eyes looking straight into Jack's. What was this boy who stood there so quietly, so calmly? Was he a friend, or was he an enemy, waiting to strike, so that the wolf dog would again feel the terror of steel trap jaws or the smothering folds of a burlap bag?

While Kata wavered, the forces within him, both dog and wolf, fought a terrible battle. Suddenly, tremblingly, Kata began to move forward. Jack held his breath. Was the wolf dog about to revert to his timber-wolf forbears and jump at his throat? Boy and animal were alone in the barn, and the boy knew he could do little to protect himself.

Or was Kata coming toward him because he wanted to? Still Jack stood, speaking quietly. "Yes, Kata, that's it, fellow. Come on, Kata, don't be scared, fellow." On the on Jack talked, hoping he showed no fear. Kata's eyes were on Jack's face, and the boy was close enough to touch the dog, but he did not move. Then Kata stretched out his muzzle and carefully sniffed at Jack's shoes. He sniffed at the boy's rolled-down jeans. Jack held himself absolutely still.

Suddenly Kata seemed satisfied, for he gave a long sigh and put his head against Jack's knee. Then he sat down on his haunches at the boy's feet.

"Oh, Kata," Jack breathed softly. "You're really my dog now, at last."

Now that Jack had won Kata's confidence, he decided it was time to let the wolf dog out of the stall. Kata would now let Jack pet him, though he still quivered at the touch of the boy's hand on his back. Kata had much to learn, the boy knew, so he began to train him slowly.

After that, the wolf dog met Jack at the door of the stall. Jack spent many hours sitting in the straw on the floor, so that Kata could lie with his head in the boy's lap. Each day as Jack put fresh straw on the floor, he and Kata played a game. Jack would pick up a big forkful of straw and throw it on top of Kata, who in turn would utter loud, mock growls and pretend to jump at Jack. At six months the wolf dog was as big as a full-grown German shepherd, and sometimes would knock Jack down without meaning to, as he was so powerful it was impossible for him to handle his own strength.

Often they kept up this mock fighting for hours, Jack continuing to shout, "That's it, boy! Try to bite me! Come on, you silly pup, you!" Kata would grab the boy's arms in his huge jaws, but he was careful to let his teeth barely touch the skin. Sometimes Jack would pretend to hide behind the bales of straw in the corner. Kata would sneak up on him, and, with a ferocious roar, jump up toward the boy's chest, teeth bared, only to lick Jack's face. It was in this rough-and-tumble play that Kata became accustomed to having the boy touch him and handle him in the way that would later be necessary when Kata's intensive training began.

Jack began to teach Kata words and the rudiments of trailing. Whenever the boy hid behind the straw bales, he always said, "Go find, Kata. Go find." At first Kata did not know what those words meant, but hearing them over and over was part of his training.

The same procedure was followed with the wolf

dog's name. Every time Jack brought his food or came to the stall, he always repeated, "Kata, Kata," until the wolf dog could not help knowing that the sound had some connection with him.

"Animals do not know the meaning of the words we use," Black-Crow told Jack, "but they learn that a certain sound, which is a word to us, is connected with a certain thing. So if you say 'food' each time you put Kata's food in front of him, he will soon learn that the sound of our word 'food' means meat.

"If you want to teach him to come instantly when you call," the Indian had continued, "put him on a leash and let him wander around at the end of it. After you say, 'Kata, come!' tug the leash until he *has* come to you. Soon he will learn that when he hears the word 'come,' a tug will follow. After a while he will not wait for the tug; he will come instantly of his own accord when you call him."

Jack used this advice to teach Kata different words. He also spent hours teaching him to stand the restraint of collar and leash. Kata would not be allowed to run free at first, even when the time came to let him out of the stall. When the collar was first put on, Kata pawed frantically at it, trying to get it off, but he soon realized that it would not budge. After a few days he paid no attention to it.

Jack practiced Kata constantly, on and then off the leash, until he was sure the wolf dog knew the command "come" so perfectly that he would always obey. Jack lavished love and affection on Kata, and the wolf dog responded, his love for the boy growing with each passing day. Kata never wagged his tail, however, a trait inherited from Red Fang, for wolves never wag their tails. But he would show his love for Jack in other ways, by putting his head on the boy's knee and by looking up at his face with adoring eyes.

Then Jack taught Kata to lie down on command. "Down, Kata," the boy said, as he pushed the surprised wolf dog down on the floor. Kata hardly knew what was happening, but quickly he understood the command, and would drop instantly to a crouch when Jack spoke.

On the day that Jack decided to begin training Kata outside the stall, the boy made sure the doors of the barn were securely shut. He also looked to see that the cows were out of the milking sheds and in the pasture, for there would be time enough later to show the cows to Kata. The boy wanted complete peace and quiet for the job he had to do, with no distractions. He went to the stall gate, and Kata greeted him with an eager whine.

"Want to come out, Kata?" Jack asked the wolf dog. "Guess you're tired of that old box stall, aren't you? Well, behave yourself now, and I'll let you out of the barn."

Although Kata did not understand what Jack was saying, he could tell from the boy's tone that something unusual was about to happen. He put his front paws up on the rail, watching eagerly. Jack opened the gate and stood back.

"Come, Kata," he said.

The wolf dog stood for a minute and then bounded out into the open part of the barn and began to run around eagerly. He sniffed in all the corners, thoroughly investigating his new domain. He ran up to Jack and poked his cold nose into the boy's hand.

"Like it?" Jack asked. "If you keep on learning so fast, you can go all over the farm pretty soon." Kata whined, as though he knew he would soon be free to go wherever he pleased. "But you've got a lot to learn first," the boy added.

The following morning when the Millers were eating breakfast, Jack brought up the subject. "Dad," he said, "I think it's time to let Kata out of the barn on a leash. He knows how to obey now, and I can handle him."

"Well, Jack," said Mr. Miller, "if you're sure he's ready for it, it's all right with me. But just remember what I told you. I can't have any trouble with him, because there are too many valuable cows on this farm to have him turn wild."

"Yes, Jack," added his mother. "Be careful. But,"

she smiled, "I think your Kata will behave himself. After all the time you've spent down in that
barn training him, he ought to!"

Jack rushed out of the dining room, Suzy trailing.
"I want to see, too, Jack," she begged. "May I come?"

She had been at the barn several times with Jack.
Kata had not seemed to mind her being there, so
Jack let her go with him.

Kata was waiting in his stall almost as though he
knew something out of the ordinary was happening. He danced around excitedly when Jack put on
the collar and leash. Jack's father and mother had
gone, too, and Mr. Miller opened the barn door.

"All right, Jack," he said, "bring him out. But,"
he continued, "I've changed my mind; bring him
out *without* the leash! If he's going to turn bad, let's
find out. You've had enough time to tame him. If
he's trustworthy I want to know it now."

Let Kata loose! Jack gasped at his father's words.
What would happen if he had not succeeded in
training Kata well enough? Did the wolf dog really
love him, or did he only appear to be affectionate
because he had been shut up in the stall, with no
choice?

Well, this was the time to find out. It was now or
never, Jack knew.

"Okay, Kata," he whispered to the wolf dog.
"Don't let me down, fellow. You've got to show Dad

that you are tame, and that you really have learned all the things you and I have practiced. Stick by me, Kata."

The big wolf dog turned his dark eyes to Jack's face and pressed his head against the boy's knee. He whined as he looked through the open door, and he licked Jack's hand. Then the boy led him outside, and stooped and unbuckled the collar and leash, letting them fall to the ground.

For a minute Kata stood and looked around the barnyard. Off in the distance he could see the outlines of the forest beyond the pastures, his beloved Great Woods stretching far to the north. His ears went up and he sniffed the fresh breeze that blew from the fir forests. Suddenly he seemed to make up his mind. He trotted across the barnyard and broke into a lope, heading for the fence. In a flash he was through the rails and racing across the pasture.

"Kata, come back!" called Jack. "Come back!" But the wolf dog did not seem to hear him and disappeared without a backward look into the long aisles between the trees.

Chapter 4

THE CATTLE DOG

ONE WEEK PASSED, and there was no sign of Kata. Mrs. Miller grew worried about Jack and tried to console him. But nothing could make the boy forget the wolf dog.

"An animal like that could never really be tamed, Jack," his father said one afternoon, when Jack had returned from another fruitless hunt for Kata.

"Maybe not, Dad, but I don't understand why he ran so fast, as if he was going somewhere special. You told me that German shepherds are one of the most faithful breeds there are, and," the boy sighed,

"I just *know* Kata has some of that in him. I know he loved me."

"I'm sure he did, too, in his own way," Mrs. Miller chimed in. "But maybe it's better he's gone. I don't believe I would ever have really trusted him, no matter how tame he seemed. He frightens me, he's so big." Secretly she thought that Kata had gone to join the wolf pack, but she didn't want to upset Jack more by saying so. "Perhaps," she said comfortingly, "he's off searching for Pierre La Touche, the hunter who raised him. A wolf dog like Kata would never forget his first master, and he might not understand that Pierre's dead."

"Maybe you're right, Mom," sighed Jack, "but I sure hope Kata's all right."

Two mornings later Jack got up earlier than usual to do his chores. It was no longer necessary to get up beforehand in order to feed Kata, but he had awakened early by a dream about the wolf dog. He had dreamed the dog was off somewhere in the north, caught in another trap.

Jack had about fifteen minutes to spare before the hired men got down to the barn to let him in. He wandered out to the big pasture and sat on the top rail of the fence, looking, as usual, off across the fields, thinking about Kata.

Suddenly he sat up straighter. Was that a movement in the scrub pine, over near the edge of the

deep woods? For a minute he couldn't see anything
more, and then, there! He saw it again! The bushes
were rustling and shaking as though something were
pushing its way through.

Oh, well, thought Jack, it's probably one of the
dairy herd, gotten loose. But then, while he stared,
a large black animal with cream-colored legs and
feet came out into the open pasture and shook himself free of the pine needles, carrying what looked
like a stick in his mouth. It was Kata! Kata, come
back!

"Here, Kata, here, fellow!" Jack shouted. The
wolf dog looked up at the sound of the boy's voice,
and began to lope rapidly across the pasture toward
him. In one bound the boy was off the fence, and
threw his arms around his pet.

"Oh, Kata," Jack said, while the dog danced
around him, "I knew you'd come back, and you
have. Where did you go; why did you run off like
that?"

Kata seemed equally pleased to see Jack, whining
eagerly and thrusting his nose into the boy's hand.
He looked very thin, and his glossy black coat was
matted with brambles and mud. Jack looked down
and saw that Kata's paws were cut and bleeding, but
the wolf dog didn't limp. He went over and nosed
at the stick he had dropped on the ground, and the
boy saw that it was an old, rotted, birchwood ax

handle, with only a small piece of the rusted axhead left fastened on.

For a minute Jack couldn't figure out what it was. Why had Kata brought this with him? Then suddenly the boy understood, and it made everything clear. Kata must have gone back up into the Great Woods, in the north, for a last search for his former master, La Touche! Here was the proof! The wolf dog must have found the place where the hunter had died, miles away from any settlement. There he had satisfied himself, once and for all, that La Touche would never need him again. He had probably found this old half-rotten ax handle in what was left of the hunter's pack, and carried it back with him, all the way to the farm!

Now, Kata picked up the birchwood handle in his strong jaws, and walked over to Jack. He waited for a minute, and when Jack made no move to take it from him, the wolf dog nudged the boy with his muzzle.

"I get it, Kata. You want me to take it. You mean I'm your master, now that you know Pierre is gone for good." Jack felt a lump rise in his throat, but he choked it back. What a thing for Kata to do! And all this time he had been wondering if Kata would come back, or if the wolf dog really loved him!

"I'll always believe in you, Kata, from now on,"

the boy said, throwing his arms around the wolf dog's neck.

He went to the barn to show his father the ax handle, and to tell him what Kata had done.

"Well, well," said Mr. Miller. "I would never have believed he'd remember how to get back up there. Guess he thought that since he'd gone back to being a dog again, he'd better make sure his old master is dead. I thought sure Kata had turned wild, like his father. You seem to have been right after all, son."

As the New Brunswick summer deepened into June, Kata and Jack spent many afternoons roaming the country beyond the pastures. Jack had promised his father that he wouldn't go too far into the fir forests, but even so he and Kata had plenty of room for their hikes. The boy also took Kata all over the farm—in the barns, in the chicken houses, and in the orchards, fields and pastures, to get the wolf dog used to every animal and activity. Jack wanted no risk of Kata's suddenly being startled by something he didn't understand.

There were more chores in the summer months, but Jack still had many hours to spend as he pleased. The boy noticed that Kata was growing rapidly, and realized that the wolf dog, too, could soon be put to work on the farm. One morning at breakfast Jack

Henry C. Pitz

asked his father if Kata could begin learning to herd the cattle.

"He's eight months old, Dad, and I think the sooner I start on the herding, the better," the boy said. "That is, if it's all right with you."

"Good idea, Jack," Mr. Miller said. "Can't have anyone idle around here, man or beast. There's too much work to be done. Kata seems obedient enough, and yes, I certainly think he's old enough for a little higher education. After breakfast we'll see about getting him started."

So it was settled. Mr. Miller had greatly enlarged his dairy herd that spring, and the need for more hired men or a careful shepherd dog was acute. At present Mr. Miller had only two hired men and Jack to help him with the herd. "I'd thought of getting a collie or two," he continued, "but if Kata's shepherd-dog blood turns out to run true, he'll be better than any collie."

The first step was comparatively simple. Jack took Kata down to the barn, not to the box stalls this time, but instead to the milking sheds. There the cows were just beginning to drift out to pasture after the morning's milking, and many of them were still standing around the water troughs. Kata had seen the cows before, of course, but always from a distance. Now Jack had to see how he would act at close range. The boy had put Kata on a leash, but he quickly saw there was no reason to worry. Kata looked at the cows with interest, then turned his attention back to his master.

A big black and white Holstein calf trotted up to investigate the boy and the wolf dog, but Kata only pricked his ears forward with interest. Jack knew that was a good sign. It would have been just as bad for Kata to ignore the cows completely as it would be to appear ferocious.

"Good boy, Kata," Jack said. "Now we'll go inside the pasture for a while." He took Kata's leash off and climbed the fence. Kata followed and cleared the rails with a bound, looking eagerly at Jack. "Just look around, fellow," the boy said, waving his hand in a circle. Kata only sniffed the ground and then sat down beside Jack, still watching the cows with interest.

"You'll do, fellow," said Jack, turning back toward the house. "We'll let the next lesson wait till tomorrow."

The next day Jack and Kata again went to the milking sheds, but this time Jack picked up a herding staff, a long stick with a hook on the end, which the men used for prodding the cows in and out of the milking stanchions. Now the boy walked among the cows with Kata on the leash, saying, "Go on, boss, go on-n-n." Those were the words the hired men used when they were driving the cows, making

the big Holsteins group together and amble slowly
through the barnyard gates. Now they were not to
have such an easy time, for Mr. Miller had said it
wouldn't hurt the cows to be Kata's training ground
for a few days. Time after time Jack rounded up
the cows, driving them in and out of the barnyard.
As he walked he repeated, "Go, boss, go-o-o," and
he constantly prodded the cows with the stick, for
Kata's benefit.

The big wolf dog could see that he was supposed
to understand something, and he strained forward
on the leash as Jack walked. "Go on, boss," Jack
said, and each time the cows began to fan out in
the pasture, the boy circled round them. As he did
so he signaled Kata forward to the end of the leash
again.

A half-hour the first day, an hour the second. By
the third day Kata was learning that the words, "Go,
boss, go," meant he and Jack were going to circle
around the cows and bunch them up. Though the
wolf dog was not yet sure of his part in this new
game, he was beginning to know what the cows were
going to do. By the fourth day Jack took Kata to
the pasture very early in the morning when the
hired men got the cows for the milking. As they
circled the herd, Kata whined.

"Want to help, don't you?" Jack smiled at the

wolf dog. "Well, you can, soon. Stay close in now and I'll let you off the leash."

The men and Jack got the herd bunched and started toward the barn. Kata stayed close to Jack, but the boy noticed his attention was all on the cows. The wolf dog's great dark eyes swept from one side of the herd to the other, and he kept his head up to test the wind.

"Kata shows all the signs of a real shepherd dog, Dad," Jack reported at breakfast. "Maybe it won't be long before he'll want to work on his own."

"Good," Mr. Miller replied. "You've got him off leash?" Jack nodded. "Fine. Now the rest is up to him. To get a good cattle dog you must let him take the initiative, and not rush him. Wait till he seems really to want to herd the cows.

"But," he continued, "the first thing Kata'll probably do is run at their heels, and you've got to watch out for that. A good cattle dog should circle in front of the herd and go to the cows' heads when they get out of line. Then the cows can see him, and they won't start running."

Jack knew the cattle must be herded slowly, for if they were pushed too fast they became nervous and upset, and this harmed their milk.

"Anyone knows a scared cow gives bad milk, Daddy," Suzy said. She had been listening to all of the training talk, and was anxious to join in the excitement. "Jack won't let Kata run them."

"You bet I won't, Suzy!" said her brother.

Along with the training in the pastures, Jack began Kata's signal training. The wolf dog already knew "come" and "down" and "go find," but that was not enough. He had to learn to run in a wide circle when Jack gave a wide sweep of his arm, and to go right or left when Jack waved in either direction. Mr. Miller had explained that those signals were very necessary for herding, in case a dog was too far away to hear the herder's voice.

To teach Kata gestures, Jack trained him on a long leash. When the boy swung his arm, he used the leash to manipulate the wolf dog in the right direction, praising him highly. Kata was quick to catch on. When Jack shouted "down," he lowered his arm sharply at the same time. Soon Kata connected the gesture with the vocal command, and in a short time he dropped at once when he saw the lowered arm, with no need for Jack's voice. He even began to look back for Jack's signals.

Kata learned to "crawl" as well, for sometimes that was the best way to move toward a nervous cow. Jack said "crawl" several times, keeping his hand low on the leash. As he moved forward he forced the wolf dog to crawl along the ground. It was difficult for Kata to inch along this way at first, but soon he got used to it and even seemed to enjoy doing his "tricks," as Suzy called them.

In the pasture, though, Kata seemed to progress no further. When they brought the cows in from the big fields he circled the herd with Jack, but never went toward the cows. He paid close attention, but that was all, and Jack began to be a little discouraged. Still, remembering his father's advice, he never tried to urge the wolf dog forward.

About three weeks after Kata's training had begun, a day dawned cold and rainy, with fitful gusts of wind. It was one of those unusual days that come occasionally in the mild New Brunswick summer. That morning Jack and the men wore rain slickers to keep off the torrents of water. The mud of the barnyard sucked at their heavy boots, forcing them to walk slowly.

The cows had ranged far out into the back pasture during the night, protecting themselves from the rain under the heavy growth of maples at the far side of the fields. It took longer than usual for the men and Jack to find them all, and when the cows were finally bunched together, they constantly broke out of the herd. They didn't want to face a long trek across the open pasture, away from the shelter of the trees. Each time the herd got started, one or two of the young heifers would break away and try to circle back to the maples. Each time Jack or one of the men would have to go after them with the prodding sticks.

Finally the herd started across the fields. As they got well into the open, the wind began to blow in strong blasts, and suddenly, directly in front of the cows, a huge solitary tree split with a loud bang that sounded like an explosion. The cows stopped, startled, eyes rolling. They began to mill around excitedly, and then one big cow broke out of line and clattered off at right angles to the herd.

"Get her, Jack, she'll have them all running!" one of the hired men shouted. Before Jack could move he heard an eager bark. It was Kata, off in a flash, straight toward the cow's heels.

"Kata, no!" Jack shouted. "Kata!" he shouted again. The big wolf dog hesitated for a second, then stopped and looked back. "Go, Kata," Jack called, signaling the wolf dog in a wide circle to the right. "Go!" The wolf dog still hesitated. Was this the same as the signals of the front lawn? His master wanted something, and all Kata knew was the training he had had in the front yard of the farmhouse. Suddenly he seemed to understand. He loped off to the right in a big circle. This time he came around in front of the cow, who slowed to a walk, faced by the whining wolf dog.

"Down, Kata," Jack shouted, and the wolf dog dropped to a crouch. "Now, CRAWL!" Kata understood. He began to creep forward toward the cow, who came to a standstill. Still the dog came on, and then, with an angry toss of her horns the cow turned around and lumbered back to the herd, Kata following behind.

Jack was so thrilled he could hardly speak. "Good boy, Kata," he managed to say, and gave the wolf dog a quick pat. There was no time for more as they still had to get the herd to the milkshed. Now, with Kata working at last, there was no more trouble. He ranged from side to side around the cows, every now and then gliding forward to head off a heifer or calf that had ideas of straying.

When the cows were safely in the milking barn, Jack could turn his attention to the wolf dog. "You did it, Kata," he said, scratching the wolf dog's ears. "I bet no boy ever had a dog as good as you." Kata licked his hand, and whined. "Want some breakfast?" Jack laughed. "You deserve it. . . . Come on, fellow, let's go! We've got some things to tell the family!"

After that Kata and Jack could go out alone for the herd, giving the hired men more time for the milking. With the spring calves coming along, it took most of the men's time just taking care of them around the barn, leaving the herding for Jack and Kata. The wolf dog improved every day, obeying Jack's hand signals at first, and then, more and more, beginning to work on his own. The herd got used to him, and soon responded to his high yipping bark, and, on hearing it, placidly obeyed the circling dog, going wherever he drove them.

Jack had hoped Kata would be a good shepherd dog, but he was astonished at the wolf dog's ability. Kata seemed almost able to think the way the cows did, knowing just how they were going to act. He seemed to sense instinctively when to circle them widely, or when to creep in close, bunching them forward through the gates.

"Oh, yes," said Mr. Miller, when Jack asked him about it. "I forget that you've never seen a real cattle dog work, but it's a beautiful sight. The sheep dogs, too. It's remarkable to watch those dogs move a herd of as many as a hundred sheep or cattle across a big field, with only one man to help them. Often the herders only signal the dogs once or twice. Why, I've seen the dogs jump on the cattle's backs and run along, to get a good view of the whole herd, before jumping down to drive them in the right direction.

"The dogs run rapidly around the flock to get them quiet," he continued, "and then bunch them. That's the tricky time. The dog has to make sure to start them in the right direction, and it bewilders them, makes them stand still, when he runs around them. Suddenly he'll drop to a crouch, the way Kata does. Inching forward, he can get the herd started so slowly that they never panic and run. Then he has them going as he wants."

"Oh, Dad," said Suzy, "will you take us to see dogs like that sometime?"

Mr. Miller smiled. "I certainly will, when I hear of a shepherd-dog trials."

"Trials?" Jack asked.

"Oh, yes," said his father. "There's a shepherd-dog club in Frontenac City, in Quebec, that holds regular trials for cattle and sheep dogs. There are big prizes. All a dog has to do to qualify is to be a working shepherd dog, on any farm. Any breed is eligible. There are usually trials every August, but I haven't heard about it this year. I'll check into it, next time I send to Howardstown for supplies. But in the meantime," he said, turning to Suzy, "we've got a pretty good shepherd dog right here for you to watch. Haven't we, Jack?"

"I'll say, Dad," the boy replied.

Chapter 5

INTO THE GREAT WOODS

O NE DAY a hunter came striding into the front
yard, bringing a message and a request from
Black-Crow. The Indian was worried about
his trap line, the hunter said, and wondered if Mr.
Miller could spare a man to take in the traps.

Usually the trappers took up their traps during
the summer months, when the fur-bearing animals
had shed their heavy winter coats and the pelts had
no value. It was a good time to oil and grease the
traps for the next winter.

But this summer, Black-Crow had been in a hurry

to reach his cabin, and had left the traps out on his trap line. He had sprung them shut the last time he had used them, but now he was afraid that game poachers or some renegade trapper might have re-set his traps. If Mr. Miller would put them in caches in the woods, the Indian could pick them up on his return down-river in the fall.

Mr. Miller told the hunter he would be glad to do this favor for Black-Crow, and even though they were busy on the farm, he could spare one of the hired men to go. The trap line ran for about thirty miles, but it was in a circle so the actual area it covered was not too great. Still, it would take at least three days to go the length of the line, as some of the traps were not well marked and would have to be located.

"Dad," Jack said, "may I go, too? The cows aren't giving as much milk, now that the calves are older, and you don't need me so much anymore. It would be wonderful to go along and take Kata. Maybe he could learn to do some woods tracking. It would help later on in trailing the cows that get out of the pasture."

Mr. Miller thought it over, and finally decided that Jack could go. "I guess Luke wouldn't mind having you along, and it would probably be good experience for both you and Kata," he said.

That night Jack and Luke, the hired man, checked

their camping equipment. They each carried a light pack, a blanket roll, and a canteen. Everything had to be in good working order. The packs contained only the essentials: frying pan, matches, salt, sugar, tea, flour, bacon and salt pork. For Kata there was dried fish, and they also took a can of fruit and some fishhooks. Luke had a belt ax, and both Jack and Luke carried hunting knives.

Luke carefully cleaned and oiled his .30-.30 rifle. "Probably won't need it," he said, "but you can't go in the Great Woods without a rifle."

With a coil of rope for the traps, their equipment was complete, and they were ready for an early start. While all these preparations were going on, Kata watched with interest. "It's almost as if he knows we're going tomorrow," Jack said, rumpling the wolf dog's head affectionately. "Don't worry, fellow, you're going, too."

The next morning Jack got up before it was light. The sky was just turning gray when he and Luke finished breakfast and shouldered their packs, ready to start. Mr. and Mrs. Miller came out on the front porch to see them off, and Mr. Miller told Jack he had better keep Kata on the leash at first.

"You want to get him in the habit of staying close to you, because once you start checking the traps there won't be time to keep an eye on him. Remember, the last time he was off in the woods he was on his own. It's not a good idea to let him range too far out of sight when you're traveling fast."

For the first few miles they hiked along the old logging trail that led to Troutville, until they got to the place where the trap line began. The first trap was the one where Jack had found Kata, and there the trail branched off the main road and headed into the backwoods.

The next few traps they found with no difficulty, following the map of the trap line that Black-Crow had sent with the hunter, on which he had marked the locations of all the traps. He had marked the kinds of traps, too; most of them were small number fours, for fox or marten, with several larger number twos for wolves.

Deeper into the wild country, where the fir forests rose on high ridges between valleys of cypress swamp, Black-Crow had carefully laid out his bear traps. In the fall season, when the bears were fat and glossy from a summer's feasting, their pelts brought high prices, so the Indian had gone to great pains to find good trapsites in the swamps. They were, however, at the point of the trail farthest away from the farm, and on the first day all of the traps that Jack and Luke hunted for were the smaller ones.

Luke showed Jack how to approach a trap carefully, first finding its chain, for all of the traps were anchored to a tree or heavy boulder by a light chain.

This prevented the captured animal from dragging the trap off on three legs, Luke explained.

When the trap was set, the chain was carefully hidden under brush or in the dirt, and the trap itself was often so skilfully hidden it was difficult to find. Though Black-Crow had sprung all of the traps, Luke said that some of them might have been reset by renegade trappers as the Indian feared. "It isn't likely," Luke said, "but we won't take any chances. We'll handle each trap as though it's set. That way if one springs suddenly when we're picking it up, it won't snap on your arm."

Each time they came to a trap, Luke would take the handle of his belt ax and bear down on the trap jaws, before unfastening the chain. By lunchtime they had found five traps, all sprung and untouched. The going had been easy so far, through heavy stands of fir and northern pine, with little underbrush.

They ate a light lunch of salt pork, washing it down with water from their canteens, and rested for a half-hour. Jack decided Kata must be used to the trail by now, so he let the wolf dog off his leash.

"He'll never go near a trap again anyway, after being caught in that first one," Luke said. "So you don't have to worry about that."

"Yes," said Jack. "Have you noticed that every

time you've picked up a trap, Kata stayed as far away as he could? He hasn't forgotten."

"He's a smart one," Luke said. "Dog like that, with so much wild strain in him, can't help but use his wits. Comes from his father who lives in the woods by his cunning."

When the half-hour was up they started on. That afternoon the trail turned sharply and swung alongside a small stream. They had to fight their way through the heavy sapling growth of the stream bank, but picked up four traps during the afternoon. They had to work more slowly because in one or two places the muskrat traps were covered over by the summer's new undergrowth. Kata ran loose, and showed no signs of ranging too far, as Jack's father had thought he might. All through the afternoon, while Luke and Jack worked, he raced back and forth through the shallows, splashing happily in the cool water. Sometimes he surprised a trout, lazing peacefully in one of the many pools of the stream. Then he bounded through the water in great leaps, barking eagerly. The great rainbow-colored fish would flash in silver arcs above the surface as they swam madly for the safety of deeper water.

"Thinks he's a regular otter, doesn't he?" Luke laughed.

Once Kata came trotting up to them, proudly bearing a fish in his mouth that had obviously been dead for some time. "Hey, Kata, that's not my idea of a good present!" Jack said, "Phew! You can just take that back where you got it!" Kata looked puzzled, and when the boy walked off the wolf dog picked up the dead fish and followed, to Luke's amusement and Jack's disgust. Finally Luke had to take the fish from Kata and bury it, while Jack said sternly, "No, Kata, *No!*" before the wolf dog would leave the hole.

By sundown they had covered twelve miles of trap line, and found fifteen traps. When they came to a large sandy shoal jutting out in the stream Luke decided they would camp there for the night. "We'll have plenty of fresh water here, and in the morning we can try a trout or two for breakfast."

Before they made camp, Luke took his ax and cut down several young spruce trees. He stripped the branches and fitted them together into a platform, high up in a gaunt old fir tree. In this cache the hired man put the traps, where they would be safe until Black-Crow could get them with his woods sledge in the fall.

After this they built a fire for supper. Jack collected the wood while Luke dug a pit in the dry sand of the shoal, and shortly they had a roaring fire going. By this time it was dark, and the little camp was filled with the tantalizing smell of frying pork and pancakes. While the food was cooking, Jack got water from the stream to boil for tea. Soon Luke called "come and get it!" but first Jack heaped a tin plate with dried fish and pork gravy for Kata. The wolf dog ate ravenously.

"Looks as though life in the Great Woods agrees with him, doesn't it, Luke?" Jack said.

"Well," Luke answered a few minutes later, "from the looks of the way you're eating, I think the woods agree with you, too!"

They planned to get up before dawn, so right after supper they cleaned the cooking things in the stream. Luke banked the fire. "I'll make it a good smoky one by sprinkling damp sand across it, in case there're any mosquitoes around," he told Jack. Then they rolled up in their blankets, and Kata curled up by Jack's side. For a few minutes the boy tried to stay awake, listening to the mysterious sounds of the night and watching the smoke curling up toward the stars.

"Just think, Kata," he whispered to the wolf dog, "we're really in the wilds now. This is Red Fang's country. . . . Wonder where he and his pack are? Hope they're nowhere around here!" His words trailed off as he got sleepier and sleepier, and in a minute his eyes closed. Kata licked Jack's hand, and with a last look at the black night around them, sighed contentedly. In a minute he too was asleep.

While it was still dark, Jack and Kata were awakened by Luke building up the fire.

"How'd you sleep?" Luke asked.

"Like a top," Jack said, "and so did Kata. Look, he's still lying right at my side." The wolf dog yawned and stretched. Jack got up and plunged into the stream for a quick bath, but the water was so cold he didn't stay long. Quickly he pulled on his clothes, his blood tingling. Luke had gone out to the point of the shoal with his fishing line, and in a few minutes he had three good-sized trout sizzling in the pan. "Boy, that smells good," Jack said. "I'm starving!"

They ate a hurried breakfast, as they had a long stretch of difficult country to cover that day, and quickly washed the frying pan and rolled the blankets. Then Luke smothered the fire carefully, and they started off up the stream bank.

It was a beautiful summer morning, and all three of them were in the best of spirits. The trees glowed bright-green, and the heavy dew made everything smell fresh and good. Soon the trail swung away from the stream, over a rise into a broad wild meadow of sweet grass. On the far side of the meadow a family of deer were feeding—a buck and a doe with two fawns. In a flash they bounded out of sight, but not before Kata had seen them and rushed off in chase. "Kata," Jack called, "come back! You can't chase the deer, even in the woods."

The wolf dog obediently turned around and came back, but he whined eagerly, and kept looking in the direction the deer had gone. "I know, old boy," Jack said, "you've got a lot of hunting blood in you. Guess it's pretty tame to have to stay here on the trail with us when you could be off after deer. But this time of year we've got to think about those fawns. They need their mother."

Partridges boomed up from the high grass under their feet, and once a big snowshoe rabbit, brown now in his summer coat, bounded away.

"There certainly are a lot of animals around here," Jack said. "Wonder why we're seeing so many more this morning than we did yesterday?"

"We're getting deeper and deeper into the real back country, that's why," Luke said. "This time of year not many trappers come this way, or hunters either for that matter, 'cause it's off any of the main trails. Animals always seem to know when it's out of season to hunt 'em or trap 'em. This part of New Brunswick we're getting into now is one of the best game ranges in the province."

They crossed the big open stretch of meadowland, and plunged into the gloom of the heavy fir forest on the far side. Here the trees were tall and thick, and stretched in great rows in every direction. The smooth ground underfoot was heavily covered with the needles, and there was little underbrush. Even so, the going was not easy, because many of the old trees had been blown down in the winter storms, and lay where they had fallen. Jack and Luke had to scramble over or around the huge deadfalls, often getting well scratched up in the process.

The ground rose steadily as they approached the ranges of hills that stretched far into the north, and they found three more traps that morning. By the middle of the day they came to a rocky knoll rising out of the forest. Below them was a wide stretch of open valley, spotted here and there with stands of timber, interspersed with cypress swamps.

"There's where Black-Crow has his bear traps," Luke said. "They're all marked on the chart he sent, but we'll probably have some trouble getting to them. Those swamps look like pretty hard going to me."

They ate lunch on the knoll, and Kata went out to the point, sniffing the breeze that blew up from the valley below. The hair rose on his back, and he whined. "What do you smell down there, Kata?" Jack said. The big wolf dog was staring down into the valley.

"No telling what he smells," Luke laughed. "But anyway," he said, shouldering his pack, "we'd better get along. There's no point wasting any more time up here when we've work to do. It's going to take us awhile to get down into the valley."

"Let's go, then," Jack said.

They started down, scrambling over the boulder-strewn slopes. As they approached the swamps the ground grew softer.

"According to the chart, the first trap is about a half-mile due north of here, on a hummock in that swamp." Luke pointed ahead. "We can find the hummock all right, 'cause it's a big stand of white pines, right in the middle of the swamp. That ought to be pretty easy to see."

Jack followed carefully in Luke's footsteps as they began to enter the swamp. Black-Crow's trail was only dimly marked and at best was very narrow. The hired man warned Jack of the dangers of stepping into a bog. Kata, with his lighter weight, could range more easily over the treacherous ground, but Jack called him in close. He couldn't risk having the wolf dog out of sight in here.

The tall cypress trees closed over their heads as they got deeper and deeper into the swamp, and once a big bull moose crashed away into the under-growth. This time of year he was growing a new set of horns, and in no mood to be disturbed. Kata growled, but made no attempt to follow the moose, and soon the crashing died away in the distance.

The ground got steadily worse, and Jack and Luke went more and more slowly. Only the turf around the roots of the big cypress trees was safe to walk on, and they had to jump over the boggy places in between. In the wide stretches of bog, they had to find old logs or thick brush to throw down for a sort of bridge.

After they had been in the swamp for some time, Kata began to growl, and pressed close at Jack's heels. "He certainly smells something, that's for sure," said Luke.

"What is it, Kata?" Jack said. "I wish you could talk."

"Lots of bear sign in here," said Luke. "This time of year they're well fed and peaceable, but he's probably got wind of a bruin, way off somewhere. Lucky they're only mean in the early spring, when they're hungry after their winter's sleep. Unless, of course, you corner a mother bear with cubs."

"Hear that, Kata? You keep close; we don't want any mother bear bothering you, or us either," Jack said.

A few minutes later the dark trees gave way to sunlight as they came out into an open glade. There, in front of them, was the big grove of white pines.

"We hit it right on the nose, didn't we, Luke?" said Jack.

"Sure did, but now we've got to find the beartrap. This part of Black-Crow's chart isn't too well-marked, so we'll have to do some hunting on our own. It says the trap is by a big deadfall, close to the roots. You circle over there," Luke said, pointing to the west, "and I'll go this way. We can meet on the far side of the grove."

The ground in the stand of pines was firm, although Jack had trouble pushing through the undergrowth. He let Kata lead the way, finding that the wolf dog instinctively took the easiest route. Each time Jack came to a fallen tree he searched the ground around the roots carefully for the bear trap. He kept steadily on, working in a big circle to the west, but with no success.

Suddenly, just as Jack was beginning to despair, he heard a sound in the distance, like a beaver slapping its tail on the water. It was so far off he could not tell what it was, but Kata heard it, too, and stood motionless, ears pricked.

"Sounds almost like the crack of a rifle, doesn't it, Kata?" Jack said. "Hey! Wait a minute! I bet it *is* a rifle! I bet Luke's found the trap, and is signaling us by the shots! Come on, Kata, let's go!"

They turned straight into the pines to the east, cutting across the middle of the hummock. Kata began to run, and Jack followed as best he could. The low-hanging branches slapped in his face and tore a big rent in his shirt sleeve, but he kept on, struggling to keep up with Kata. Every now and then the wolf dog stopped and waited while the boy caught up, and then the dog bounded on.

In a few minutes they came to the far side of the pines, just about where Jack thought he had heard the shots. There was no sign of Luke. "This is where those shots came from, I know," he said to Kata. "Maybe if I shout he'll hear me and answer."

"Luke, hey-y-y, Luke," the boy called. Still there was no answer. "Come on, Kata, we'll have to hunt. Maybe we can use your cattle training. Go find, Kata, go find." The boy waved his arm in a wide circle, in the same way he signaled the wolf dog to go after the cows at the farm. After watching him a moment, Kata seemed to understand, and with a loud bark he bounded off into the trees. Jack sat down on a log to wait, not wanting to go too far from the place where Kata had last seen him.

The minutes dragged by. A wood thrush sang in a pine nearby, but otherwise all was still.

Suddenly, Jack sat bolt upright. Wasn't that Kata barking in the distance? He listened hard, and again the sound came. This time he recognized Kata, barking wildly. Jack jumped up and ran toward the sound, through a thick growth of the pine trees.

After about a hundred yards he came to a tiny glade with a big deadfall in the middle. There he saw Kata, standing at the foot of the fallen tree. Beside him was the motionless form of Luke. The hired man's foot was held deep in the deadly grip of the very bear trap they had been trying to find!

Jack ran forward. "Oh, Kata," he exclaimed, "what are we going to do now?"

Chapter 6

KATA TO THE RESCUE

IN A FEW minutes Luke stirred slowly. Then, with a groan of pain, he opened his eyes. Jack knelt down beside him, trying to see how the hired man's leg was caught.

"How bad does it look, Jack?" Luke asked, when he was able to speak.

"I don't know, but I'm going to try to get a stick to use as a lever and pry open the trap jaws."

"No, you better not. If the lever should slip, the jaws would snap back harder than ever, and my leg would be done for. If it isn't already." Luke tried to sit up, but the effort made his face turn gray with pain and he had to lie down again, gasping.

Jack unbuckled his canteen and held it to the man's lips. "There isn't much left, but there must be a clear stream in these pines. Drink it all, Luke," the boy urged. Kata ran around, whining and trying to lick Luke's face. The big wolf dog could tell that something was wrong.

Jack told Luke how he had heard the report of the gun and had come running to find him, but had gotten no answer when he called.

"Guess I kind of fainted from the pain," Luke said. "Last thing I remember was firing the rifle, hoping you'd hear it and come find me. Good thing Kata's got such a good nose."

"It sure is," Jack said. "I wouldn't have known where to look, when I didn't find you where I thought I heard those shots."

"Well, he found me, anyway, and now we've got to decide what to do next. There ought to be some way to spring this trap, if I can help you. Two of us'd be strong enough to hold the jaws open."

Again the hired man tried to sit up, and again he had to fall back, weak from pain. His leg was so doubled under him that he could barely move without causing agony. "Guess I'll just have to stay this way," he grinned weakly at Jack, "till we decide how to open the trap."

Jack took the pack from Luke's back, and put the rolled blanket under the man's head to make him more comfortable. They made plans for the night, as it was getting dark fast. The searching had taken a long time.

"Jack," said Luke a little later, "I've been thinking. I can't sit up, and you can't open the trap by yourself. I don't see any way to open it. Tomorrow you'll have to go and get help. With Kata you can make it all right."

"But, Luke," Jack protested. "I can't leave you here. Besides, I'm not sure I can find the trail." The boy was almost sure he could find the way back, but he didn't want to leave Luke. If the hired man thought Jack couldn't find the trail, he wouldn't make him go. "Even if Kata does know the way back to the farm, that doesn't mean he'd take me there. He's a wolf dog, born in these woods, and it's just as much home to him as the farm is."

"With my compass, and the map, you can make it all right," Luke said. "Anyway, I'll be okay here till you bring help.

"We won't talk about it any more tonight," the hired man said as he saw Jack open his mouth to protest again. "But I want you to go."

The idea of leaving Luke lying alone, flat on his back in the middle of the cypress swamp, filled the boy with anxiety. It was a long way to the farm,

The
heaped
then tι
leg loι
groggy
cause l
head, a
or Suzy
off to fi
a sprin
sleeve ι
he wer
cloth.
"Th:
Jack
to stay
that Lι
pening
nothin{
to the
down a
"Kat
do you
looked
the boy
was it?
"Go

and there was no telling what might happen to Luke while Jack was gone.

He said nothing more while he tried to make Luke comfortable for the night, talking cheerfully instead about other things to take Luke's mind off the pain. He built a fire the way Luke had showed him, being very careful in such a dry grove of trees. Then he cooked a supper of tea and meat. Neither of them ate very much, and not even Kata seemed to be hungry.

After supper Luke started to tremble with a chill and Jack put his own blanket over the man. Then the boy curled up on the pine needles close to the fire to keep warm. Kata lay down beside him.

Just as Jack was falling asleep he was suddenly awakened by a growl from the wolf dog. Beyond the circle of firelight the woods were black as pitch. Jack strained his ears to listen. Nothing stirred, but still Kata growled, rumbling low in his throat. Jack put his hand on the dog's neck, and felt the hair rise stiffly.

Luke was asleep, muttering and tossing fitfully from the pain, but Jack crawled over and woke him. "What do you think it could be, Luke?" he asked, after telling the injured man about Kata's uneasiness.

"Probably some lynx, or maybe even a cougar. Or could be a bear. . . . There're lots of them around here. Anyway, whatever it is, it won't come near the

fire, so don't worry. Keep Kata close to you, and go on to sleep.''

Jack went back to his side of the fire and lay down, but he didn't close his eyes. He thought about how it would be for Luke, lying there tomorrow night all by himself, with no Kata to growl and warn him of any animals nearby.

Besides, Jack thought, even if I leave him a good supply of firewood, how'll he sit up and feed the fire during the night? The boy lay there, looking at the pine branches above him, and wondered what to do. "No," he muttered to himself. "I won't leave him, that's all. I can't. There's no telling what would happen if he's left all by himself here. I just won't leave him. You'll have to go, Kata," he said, turning to the wolf dog. Kata lay with his head on his paws, staring into the flickering fire. His growls had subsided, and at the sound of Jack's urgent voice he looked up and whined.

"You'll have to go, fellow," the boy repeated. "I *know* you can find your way back, if you want to! You've got to do it for Luke, and for me!"

Kata put one paw on the boy's lap. He licked Jack's face, and whined again. "I think you will, too, Kata," the boy said. Then, having satisfied himself with a plan for action, he rolled over and went to sleep.

The next morning Jack was up at dawn. He heaped more wood on the fire, fixed breakfast, and then turned his attention to Luke. The hired man's leg looked swollen and purple, and he seemed groggy. He asked Jack to take the blanket away because he felt hot, and when Jack felt Luke's forehead, as he had seen his mother do when either he or Suzy was sick, it was burning with fever. He went off to find fresh water, and in a short time discovered a spring in a nearby thicket. The boy tore off the sleeve of his shirt and dipped it in the water. Then he went back and wiped Luke's face with the cool cloth.

"That feels better," Luke said, and dozed off again.

Jack had been worried about telling Luke his plan to stay and send only Kata for help, but he saw now that Luke was so ill he hardly knew what was happening. With Luke safely asleep again there was nothing to stop Jack, so he called Kata and walked to the edge of the clearing by the deadfall. He sat down and put his hand on Kata's head.

"Kata," he said, "I want you to go home. Home, do you understand? Go home, Kata!" The wolf dog looked at Jack with his great dark eyes. He realized the boy was trying to tell him something, but what was it?

"Go find home, Kata!" The big wolf dog gave

one quick bark, and then, without another sound, turned and headed into the swamp. He paused once to look back, before disappearing from sight.

With a sigh Jack went back to the camp. Luke slept on, but his face looked flushed and his leg was still angry and swollen.

"I sure hope Kata hurries," Jack said to himself.

The day passed slowly, for once Jack had made Luke as comfortable as possible, he had nothing else to do. He didn't want to leave the hired man long enough to go exploring, and besides, there was no real reason to go far from the camp. Everything they needed was right there. Even the water was close, and Jack knew that Luke had brought enough food for at least two more days. The hired man had explained that it was always a good plan to take along an extra day's supply of food on even a short camping trip.

Luke woke up for a while in the afternoon. Jack made him some tea, which was all he would take. Luke said little about his leg, but Jack could tell it hurt more than ever, for Luke turned pale every time he moved. The trap jaws were buried almost to the bone, making the surrounding flesh ooze with an ugly infection.

In the afternoon Jack busied himself by cleaning up the camp and collecting wood for the night's fire.

Then he found a flint rock and sharpened both hunting knives and the belt ax, and cleaned the rifle. After that he cut some balsam to make himself a bed, for Luke seemed cold again and needed both of the blankets.

By the time the boy finished it was almost dark. He made supper, trying to cook some pancakes from the leftover flour, and, though they were not as good as those Luke made, the hired man ate part of one. "Tastes pretty good, boy," he smiled at Jack. "You're getting to be a real woodsman."

After supper he seemed to feel better for a while, but his leg appeared more swollen. Jack packed it in a wet cloth to try to bring the swelling down.

"Won't be long now before they come for us," the boy said, trying to sound cheerful. He had told the hired man at lunchtime about sending Kata on alone. Luke was upset, but it was too late to do anything about it, so he accepted matters as gracefully as he could under the circumstances.

Soon after supper Jack got ready for the night. He cleaned up the cooking things in the spring, and settled down on his balsam bed. He lay for a long time before he went to sleep, wondering how Kata was faring. Had the wolf dog headed straight for the farm? Or was it possible he might still have too much of Red Fang's blood and revert back to the wild and join the wolf pack? The country Kata had to cross on his way to the farm was very wild, as Jack had seen, and the wolf dog would have many hours to feel the call of the Great Woods.

Well, it all depends on Kata, Jack said to himself, but I'll never really doubt him again, after the way he came back from his search for Pierre La Touche. He'll get there.

The fire flickered low. Once there was a crashing in a thicket far back in the pines, and Jack sat bolt upright, straining to see. After a moment the crashing stopped, and soon nothing disturbed the silence of the night. Finally, exhausted, the boy fell asleep.

That morning, when Kata plunged into the cypress swamp, he headed straight south. He was going in the direction of the knoll in the fir forest where Jack and Luke first had seen the valley. At first the going was fairly easy, for the ground was still good on the outskirts of the pine hummock. But as he got deeper into the swamp, the wolf dog found himself having to stop and circle widely around dangerous bogs more and more often.

Once he halted on a rock in the middle of a sluggish bog and hesitated, wondering which way to go next. All around him was the treacherous, sucking mud, and there seemed to be no way to go forward safely.

He put one paw tentatively on what looked like

a solid place, with tall grass growing on it. Quickly he drew his paw back as he felt the squishy mud under the grass. It was not growing on solid ground at all, but in the mud. Finally he saw an old log about ten feet away, near the base of a big tree, and he decided to jump to it.

There was no room for a running start, and the wolf dog paused a minute longer, judging the distance. Then he crouched, drawing his hindquarters under him, and took one step forward. He thrust his powerful hind legs backward against the rock and jumped, his body arching through the air, then landed just short of the log in the sucking mud. As he felt himself dragged down, Kata made one last mighty surge forward and threw his forelegs onto the old log. He had made it!

He stood for a minute on the log, panting, before starting on again. Clearly in his mind were Jack's last words, "Go find home, Kata!" and he could sense his master was worried. Now he had only one thought, and that was to do Jack's bidding. He had not understood all of the words Jack had said to him, but he knew the word for "home" and he knew what "go find" meant. To Kata, it was clear what the boy wanted, and in his deep love for Jack he pressed forward to obey gladly.

When Jack and Luke had come into the valley the wild animals had stayed hidden, well away from the dreaded men. Now, alone, Kata saw the teeming life of the forest all around him. Unconsciously he reverted to the furtive ways of the forest dwellers, taking advantage of every cover, gliding silent as a shadow through the gloom of the swamp.

The furred and feathered denizens of the Great Woods went about their struggles for survival— hunting and playing, living and dying, undisturbed by the wolf dog's passing. He galloped across enticing game trails, and once he saw a cow moose and her calf straddling a young sapling to reach the tender topmost leaves. But Kata held unswervingly to his course.

Galloping under a low-hanging hemlock branch, he suddenly caught the scent of lynx, and looked upward. There, on the branch above, crouched the big gray cat. His yellow eyes glittered and his small tufted ears were twitching in anger. For a minute they silently faced each other, the dog and the lynx, members of two clans that had been enemies since time immemorial.

The lynx dug his claws into the bark of the branch and hissed at the wolf dog in a fury of hatred. Kata's hackles rose, his lips curled back from his teeth in a snarl. But into his brain came Jack's command, "Go home, Kata!" and the wolf dog remembered his errand. He growled low, but he turned away, and went on.

As Kata bounded out of sight among the hemlocks, the lynx vented his fury with a screech of rage. Then he padded off to seek another thicket, for he knew his angry yowl had warned his prey into their burrows, quivering with fear.

Kata soon forgot his thwarted animosity toward the lynx, for he had reached the edge of the swamp. Scrambling up the rocky walls of the valley, he entered the fir forest above. Here the going was better, but the wolf dog was getting tired, for he had run far and fast. His tongue was hanging out and he breathed hard. Now he slowed from the lope of the wolf to the trot of the German shepherd, swinging easily into a gait that had been bred in the shepherd dogs hundreds of years ago for their work of following the flocks.

By the early afternoon Kata had crossed the wild meadow and come to the stream, where just two days before he had splashed so happily in the water. This time he paused only long enough to drink thirstily from its cool waters. The heavy brush of the stream bank was hard going, and after an hour of scrambling around thickets and through the briers he stopped to rest for a few minutes, lying half in a pool of water. He panted hard, and lapped the water eagerly to slake his burning thirst. Rested, he got to his feet and soon came to the place where the trail swung into the woods again. Under the pine trees the underbrush was less heavy and he could keep a steady pace.

Following an old game trail, Kata's attention was caught by a cracking twig in a deep thicket some yards off the trail. The wolf dog stopped, ears forward, testing the air with his nose, but the noise had ceased. He started on, but then the noise came again and he turned aside to investigate.

The wolf dog glided across a sun-dappled open glade to the edge of the thicket, where again he stopped to listen and sniff the air. This time he caught a scent that made him growl low in his throat. Again the hackles rose on his neck, and he dropped to a crouch, taking cover behind every tree as he crept forward. The thicket gave way to the open bank of a small creek, and Kata peered down at the pool that widened below. On the edge was a large red weasel, possessively crouched over a freshly killed trout, one forepaw on the still thrashing fish.

The weasel had scented Kata, and was snarling his defiance as the big wolf dog appeared.

Kata stood motionless, watching. This was none of his affair. He was about to turn away when the weasel, that most bloodthirsty of all wild creatures, came darting up the bank to launch himself straight at the wolf dog's throat!

The ferocious attack barely missed Kata's jugular

vein, as the wolf dog, like lightning, shifted to one side. Instead, the weasel fastened his teeth in the thick hair and muscles of Kata's neck and held on. The bank echoed with their snarls as the two battled desperately, rolling over and over among the pine needles. Kata made a violent attempt to shake the little animal loose, for the weasel was so close to the wolf dog's head that Kata could not bring his own fangs into play.

Then came Kata's opportunity. His powerful neck muscles bulging with effort, he flung himself on the ground on top of his opponent. Twisting under the wolf dog's weight, the weasel loosened his grip to get a better hold.

That instant was enough. Kata jerked his whole body sideways, and the weasel slipped to the ground. Before he could renew the attack, Kata leaped clear over him, and this time, when the red demon ran forward, Kata was ready. One crunch of the wolf dog's powerful jaws and the weasel writhed on the ground, still snarling. Kata tossed him into the air, and with a snap slammed the now beaten creature to the earth. In a moment the weasel lay still.

Kata made sure he was dead, then trotted down the creek bank to the pool. The weasel's prize, the fish, lay where he had left it, only partly eaten. Now the spoils were Kata's. He was hungry, and in one gulp finished the meal.

Then the wolf dog drank deeply from the amber pool, smelling the cool dampness of the mossy banks. A breeze blew across the water, carrying the pungent scent of the Great Woods—wild, mysterious, and vaguely disturbing.

Memories stirred Kata; memories of roaming through deep forests and sun-filled meadows, or following streams such as this in search of prey. He too, like the weasel lying dead on the bank, had once crouched over a freshly killed rabbit, to drink deep of its warm blood. He too had prowled through the black forest nights with only the voices of the wild for company, or the distant stars that looked down on his lair under a fallen tree.

The life on the farm had nearly blotted out the young wolf dog's early months, but now he had tasted blood again, the blood of a foe that he had fought fairly and to the death. Through his veins surged the instincts of generations of primitive wolves.

He raised his dripping head from the water, and sniffed long and questingly of the breeze. What new trails of the wild lay across that stream, what dark spruce thickets called beyond the far-off hills? The wolf dog whined. He could not understand the unrest that was in him.

Somewhere out there, he knew, was the wolf pack, though he had never seen them. Almost as if he could hear their long-drawn howls, as they raced hard on the trail of a fleeing moose, the wolf dog threw back his head and answered, his howl echoing through the sunny clearing in an agony of unknown longing.

In the silence that followed there was no answer, and the spell was broken. The voice of the wolf dog had replied to the call of the wolf pack, but the heart of Kata belonged to his master.

He drank once more from the pool and sniffed at the dead weasel. Then without stopping for a backward look, he bounded up the bank to the trail, and loped steadily on his way.

In another hour he had come to the old logging road that led from the farm to the village of Troutville, and here the going was comparatively easy. Kata went more slowly, for he was very tired. He had been on the trail since the early morning with hardly a moment's pause, and his neck hurt badly where the weasel's fangs had torn his flesh. The blood dripped down his shoulder in a slow trickle, but he did not stop to lick it off.

Just before sunset Kata came to the outer edge of the farm. With renewed energy he trotted toward the house, and came up to the front porch. Inside, the lights blazed, for the family was eating supper.

Kata went to the front door and scratched it, whining. When this got no response he began to bark, loudly and urgently. Mr. Miller came to the door, and immediately recognized Kata.

"Why, Kata, what are you doing here?" he said. "Where are Jack and Luke? What'd you do, come on ahead of them to get your dinner?"

Mrs. Miller had appeared at the door by this time, followed by Suzy, and they both greeted the wolf dog. Mr. Miller held open the door, but Kata would not go inside. Wasn't there any way he could make them understand?

He barked again, and this time he grabbed hold of Mr. Miller's sleeve and tried to pull him toward the porch steps.

"I think the animal has gone crazy," Mr. Miller said, jerking his arm away from Kata's grip. "What do you suppose is wrong with him?"

"You know, I do believe he's upset about something," Mrs. Miller said. "Look at the way he keeps barking, and . . . why, Bob! Look at the blood on his neck! He's hurt!"

"So he is," Mr. Miller said. "Maybe you're right; something must be wrong." He peered out toward the entrance to the farm, and the empty road. "That's funny, there's still no sign of Jack and Luke. I think we'd better see what Kata wants."

He went back into the house for his flashlight and a leash, while Kata waited outside, still barking impatiently. In a minute he came out again, and followed the wolf dog down the steps toward the farm gates. When he saw that Kata was leading him toward the logging road, he slowed down.

"Something really *is* wrong, isn't there, Kata old boy?" Mr. Miller said to the wolf dog. "But no matter what it is, we'll have to go back to the house. If anything has happened to Jack and Luke out there in the Great Woods, I can't go off in the dark like this to hunt for them, even with you to lead the way." He peered ahead. "There's no telling how far off they are, and that bush is too thick to start through at night, even with a flashlight. Come on, we'll have to go back and wait till morning."

Kata paid no attention and tried to grab Mr. Miller's sleeve again. This time the man was ready for him and caught the wolf dog by the neck. Quickly slipping a leash over Kata's head, he started back for the farmhouse.

"I'm sorry, Kata," he said, "but this time you'll have to obey me. I know how much you want to get back to wherever Jack is, but my way is best. We'll go as soon as it's light enough to see."

Though he whined and tried to pull back on the leash, there was nothing for Kata to do but follow Mr. Miller. Jack's father led the wolf dog into the house, and shut him up in the kitchen.

"You'll be better off in there, till morning," he told the dog.

Mrs. Miller fixed Kata a big bowl of table scraps left over from dinner, but he would not eat. "Poor Kata," she said, "I'll wash that wound. It looks as though you've been in a fight."

She got a basin of water, gently sponged the blood from Kata's neck, and covered the ragged bite with ointment. Then the wolf dog restlessly paced the kitchen floor until finally, realizing that it was useless to try to get out of the house, he curled up in a corner and lay down, whining softly.

Early in the morning Mr. Miller filled a light rucksack with food and a first-aid kit. At the last minute he picked up his rifle. He did not want to upset Jack's mother, but he felt it best to be prepared for whatever might happen. "Don't worry, dear," he told Mrs. Miller, "I'm sure they're all right. Probably just got held up somewhere, and Kata came on back to the farm because he was restless."

In the kitchen Kata was still pacing around the room, and the wolf dog seemed more upset than ever.

"Okay, old boy," Mr. Miller said. "We're leaving right now." He put the leash on the wolf dog and opened the door. Kata rushed through and began to strain forward, pulling Mr. Miller as fast as he would go.

As they went through the front yard Jack's father

stopped only long enough to call the other hired man from the dairy barn to come with him. He felt it best to have another man along, in case of real trouble.

Then he turned to Kata and said, "All right, Kata, it's your lead now. Find Jack, boy, take us to Jack!"

The wolf dog gave an eager bark, and, pulling steadily on the leash, led the two men down the old logging road until they came to the trap-line trail crossing. Here he stopped, barked again, and turned into the dim green of the forest.

Back in the camp in the pines, Jack was worried. That morning when he woke up he couldn't even make Luke drink any tea, and the hired man was becoming delirious. He mumbled as he dozed, and occasionally cried out. His leg seemed to be throbbing unbearably from the pain and looked too swollen to touch. Jack had no medicine of any kind, only the damp cloth which he kept on Luke's forehead. The fever did not lessen, but Jack did not know what else to do.

"Wonder why Luke didn't bring a first-aid kit," the boy said to himself. "Guess he forgot it. Anyway, even if I had a first-aid kit, I couldn't open the trap. That's the most important thing." Jack knew the leg was infected from the steel jaws of the trap, and this caused the steady swelling. For the hundredth time since he had sent Kata off, Jack wondered whether the wolf dog had gotten back to the farm. Then he thought of something else. Would his father understand, and come back with Kata to find them?

"I guess all I can do is hope," he muttered as he put more wood on the fire. He had decided he would keep the fire going day and night, not only for protection, but to serve as a beacon to anyone who might be searching for them.

The day passed slowly. Around four o'clock dark storm clouds began to gather, and by early dusk the rain was falling, first lightly and then in a heavy downpour. Thunder rumbled in the distance, and once or twice there were flashes of lightning on the horizon. Jack drew the blankets closer over Luke, for the air was damp and almost cold from the sudden summer storm.

The boy huddled under a tree, pulling the balsam boughs of his bed around him to try to keep some of the water off. It seemed useless to hope for rescue now, as the rain quickly put out the fire and soaked the extra wood that Jack had collected. Still the boy kept watching the swamp to the south, hoping to see the flare of torches, or the steady beam of a flashlight. If only someone, anyone, would come to rescue them! How he longed for the comforting warmth of Kata's presence!

After a while Luke's restless groaning quieted. Jack hoped the hired man was sleeping soundly, for only sleep could blot out the pain. Now all was quiet but for the steady downpour of the rain and the dripping leaves underneath the trees. The sound of the rain lulled Jack, and his head nodded. He propped his back against the tree, and soon fell into a light doze.

The boy awakened suddenly, and for a minute did not know where he was. Then he remembered, and hunched himself deeper against the tree trunk, but held his head up to keep from going back to sleep. What had made him wake up so suddenly? Had he heard something, a sound, perhaps, far off in the distance?

He listened, but there was nothing. No, it must have been his imagination.

But there! There *was* a sound! The sound he had heard in his sleep and that had awakened him! It was the muffled, distant barking of a dog. A dog! Could it be . . .? Yes!

For again the bark came, this time closer. There could be no mistaking it. It was Kata, coming from the swamp!

A pang of fear made Jack shiver. Suppose Kata was alone? Suppose he hadn't gone back to the farm at all? If he hadn't, then Jack knew he would never get Luke out alone.

The boy stood up, trying to see through the rain and the dark, but he could not make out anything more than ten feet away. The night was pitch-black, and he wondered if Kata would be able to find the campsite. He wished desperately for the fire, but the wood was too wet even to try building another one; it would just waste the precious matches.

The bark sounded again, much nearer now. Jack began to shout at the top of his lungs. "Kata, here!" he cried. "Here, fellow!" His voice echoed off into the swamp, but the barking was louder, and Jack could tell the wolf dog had heard him.

The boy kept calling, guiding the dog forward. Suddenly he saw the distant glow of flashlights. That meant people, probably his father, were with Kata. Jack let out his breath in a great sigh of relief.

"Luke!" he cried. "They're here. Kata's brought help!"

Rapidly the lights came nearer, occasionally circling what Jack knew must be the bogs of the swamp, and in a few minutes he could see Kata leading Mr. Miller and the other hired man. They stepped onto the firm ground of the pine grove, and Jack fell to his knees to bury his face in Kata's ruff.

"Good boy," was all he whispered, but for the wolf dog it was enough.

Chapter 7

NARROW ESCAPE

QUICKLY Mr. Miller and the other hired man pried open the jaws of the trap. It was a fairly simple matter for the two men, one gently moving Luke's leg out while the other held the lever tightly, giving it no chance to spring shut.

Then, using the flashlights, they searched for dry wood, hidden away in hollows and under dense thickets. Jack used his hands to claw and scrape at the wet pine needles under the old fire site, until he had bared a dry shallow depression for a new fire. They used dry punk from great fallen pine trunks for tinder, and struck the matches. Finally, hissing and smoking, the flame caught. Luke opened his eyes in its warm and cozy light, and recognized Mr. Miller.

"Jack's done a good job," he whispered, and dozed off again.

"It was Kata," Jack said, and his father smiled.

"Yes, but seems to me it was pretty brave of you to send him, son." Mr. Miller looked around. "And you've made a good camp here."

Jack flushed at the praise, and kept his face out of the light while he helped put the dried-out blankets on the spruce boughs. Then they all turned in, to wait for daylight.

At sunrise, Mr. Miller cut young saplings, and Jack helped the other hired man fashion them into a woods sledge. Luke was still feverish, and they hurried as fast as they could, packing up the camp, trampling the fire, and lifting him onto the sledge.

Kata bounded around, seemingly oblivious to the pain from his neck wound. But fresh blood was beginning to ooze from it again, and Jack was worried. Suppose it became infected, like Luke's leg? He had no more bandages; the only thing they could do was travel as rapidly as possible. Finally they reached the farm, late in the afternoon.

Mrs. Miller took charge at once. She put Luke to bed, shut Kata in the kitchen, and used the same treatment on them both. She soaked the wounds with hot poultices to draw out the infection, cleaned and changed the bandages every hour, and gave Luke hot soup and Kata all the water he would drink. Jack helped her, and then sat on the floor beside Kata to keep the great wolf dog quiet. Now and again he put his hand on the dog's head, and rumpled his ears.

"Good boy, good boy, Kata," he whispered, and the wolf dog licked his hand.

In a few days, thanks to the prompt rescue and Mrs. Miller's constant nursing, Luke and Kata were much improved. Luke's leg was still open and raw, but the infection was subsiding nicely, and the swelling was nearly gone. He would have to walk with a cane for a while, but otherwise it was only a matter of time and rest before his leg would be as good as new.

Kata, too, was almost well. The wound in his neck was closed, for he was healthy and strong, and his clean blood purged the poison quickly. The time in the swamp seemed like a bad dream now, almost as if it had never happened. Life was back to normal, and again the farm work swung into its regular routine.

One day at dinner Mr. Miller said he had a surprise.

"I have heard that the shepherd-dog trials are to be held next week, in Frontenac City," he said. "I am taking the whole family to see them! This summer I can afford to leave the farm in Luke's competent hands for a short time, and we will stay with your grandmother there. She hasn't seen you since you were too young to remember."

Jack and Suzy could hardly finish their dinner from the excitement. They were going to Frontenac City! It was far, far to the west, all the way into another province, and they had never been so far from home before. This would be the first time they had visited their grandmother. There had always been school, or too much to do on the farm for their father to leave.

Then Jack had an idea, and the very thought made him put down his knife and fork. Perhaps he could take Kata and enter him in the shepherd-dog trials! He looked at his father, wondering how to bring it up.

"What's the matter, Jack?" his mother asked.

It was now or never.

"I was wondering, Dad . . . Well . . . could I take Kata?" He rushed on. "And enter him in the competition? He's just about perfect now in herding the cattle. Maybe he could win a prize."

Mr. Miller considered. Jack held his breath.

"Well," his father spoke at last, "I don't see why not. He certainly is a good herder, and who knows?

He might win something. It would be good experience at any rate—for him and for you, too.

"Of course Kata isn't used to anything but the farm and the woods," Mr. Miller continued before the boy could speak. "He may not take to the city; it might bewilder him so much he'll get confused and forget his training. But we can see what happens. He deserves a chance after the way he rescued you and Luke."

So it was settled. Kata was to enter the shepherd-dog trials!

Jack excused himself as soon as he could and rushed into the yard, whooping with sheer joy. Kata barked and ran beside him, infected by Jack's wild exuberance.

"Okay, fellow." The boy sat down suddenly, throwing his arms around the big wolf dog. "Now we must get to work. We've got to practice until you're really perfect!"

Mr. Miller told Jack exactly what the trials rules were, for he had seen many of the shepherd-dog trials when he lived in Frontenac City as a young man.

"Kata will have to do mostly what he does right here, when he is helping you and the men round up the cows," he told Jack. "The main difference will be the excitement, and the crowds of people.

There will be a large field they call the 'working area,' and in the middle is a big pen. The dogs work with either sheep or cattle, depending on which they are used to."

He went on to explain that the dogs must bring the herd all the way across the entire length of the field, keeping them well bunched and not moving too fast. Then, on a signal from the handler, the dog must drive the cows into the pen.

"That won't be hard for Kata, because it's just what he does here every day, when he drives the cows through the barnyard gates. The pen at the trials will be just about the same size as our milkshed yard."

So the boy and Kata went to work harder than ever before. Every day, as usual, they went with the hired men to bring in the cows. Jack trained Kata until the wolf dog's herding ability, already instinctive, grew until he seemed to sense the cows' every move, and be there ahead of them. He also seemed to know what Jack's signals would be almost before the boy gave them. For the bond between the boy and the wolf dog, already strong, had tightened into steel since the ordeal in the cedar swamps, and now they worked together as though unseen currents flowed between their minds and hearts.

One warm morning they finished a training session early, and Jack went to sit on the front porch where Suzy and his mother were shelling beans for dinner. Kata lay in a patch of sunlight in the front yard, his head on his paws. Nearby, Suzy's kitten chased its tail in high good spirits at the warm weather, and Kata watched her lazily, though his ears were pricked toward his master on the porch. Jack and Suzy were eagerly discussing Kata's chances in the coming trials, and Jack was telling her how well the wolf dog had worked that morning.

"Kata doesn't look a bit worried," Mrs. Miller laughed, pointing to the big wolf dog lying in the sun.

"Guess he knows he's good," Jack said proudly.

"Jack," said Suzy, "where's my kitten? She was playing in the yard, and now I don't see her!"

"Gosh, Suzy, how would I know? She's probably under the porch, hunting for field mice," Jack said.

"She wouldn't go far," Mrs. Miller added. "Hurry up with those beans; I've got dinner to cook and the washing to do first."

The children turned diligently to their work, and soon the big pan of glistening beans was full, the empty hulls gathered for the pig troughs.

Suzy's kitten did not appear. "Please, Jack, help me find her," Suzy begged. "Okay, Suzy," the boy said. They hunted under the porch and all around the front yard, and under the bushes that lined the base of the house.

"Where is she, Kata?" Jack said. "She was right here with you a little while ago." The wolf dog sniffed around, but seemed to pay little attention to the search. Jack did not want to give him the command "go find," for fear it would interfere with the wolf dog's cattle training. That was too important now, just before the trials.

"You and I'll find her," he told Suzy. "She's just wandered off somewhere, and she'll be back before you know it. Cats like to prowl around."

"But I want my kitty now!" wailed Suzy. "Can we go down around the barnyard and look for her? Maybe she's gone to see the baby chickens."

"Sure, Suzy. We'll take a look. Come on, Kata."

The kitten was nowhere to be seen in the barnyard, so the children started back to the house, as it was nearly time for dinner. As they were going through the barnyard gate, Mr. Miller came out of the barn and called to Jack. "Come here a minute, please, Jack. I want you to wash some of these milk pails; they're all piled up right inside the barn door."

"Sure, Dad," said Jack. "Suzy, you take Kata and go on up to the house, and I'll be up later. Your kitty's probably home by now." He turned to the wolf dog. "Go with Suzy, Kata." The wolf dog pressed close to Jack's leg, not wanting to go, but he knew he must obey. Leaving his master for even a single moment was not to Kata's liking. But when Jack repeated his command to "go with Suzy," the wolf dog reluctantly followed the little girl, who wandered off across the barnyard, still calling her kitten.

Jack went into the barn and picked up the empty pails, piling them in the big tubs that were there for that purpose. He worked busily, scrubbing the pails until they gleamed with cleanliness. When he finished the washing, he stacked them in neat rows in the milking shed, all ready for the evening's milking, and then started up the hill toward the house. The boy walked along whistling, thinking of the coming shepherd-dog trials. He wondered how Kata would react to all the excitement of the trials and to the city, and if the wolf dog would win a prize. There would be a great many experienced shepherd dogs there, Jack knew, but he had great faith in Kata's ability and in the wolf dog's desire to obey the boy's commands always.

When Jack got to the house, Suzy and Kata were nowhere to be seen. Suzy's probably in the kitchen with Mother, the boy said to himself. He whistled for Kata, but there was no response. Then he cupped his hands and called, "Kata, come here!"

In a minute he walked to the side of the front porch and saw Kata bounding up the hill from the direction of the barnyard.

"Where have you been, old fellow, looking for me?" Jack smiled at his pet's delight in seeing him, and began to rumple Kata's ears. He thumped Kata's ribs, and the big wolf dog, knowing it was a game, leaped in a growling rush at the boy's arm. Suddenly their play was interrupted by a sound that froze Jack in his tracks. It was Suzy's voice, but instead of coming from the house, it came from the pasture behind the big barn. And she was screaming!

Jack saw his father and Luke dash out of the milksheds. He heard Mr. Miller shout, with a terrible note of fear in his voice, "The bull! The bull is in that pasture! Get the nose rings, Luke, and a pitchfork! Hurry!" As he spoke he broke into a dead run toward the pasture gate.

The farmhouse was on a rise of ground above the barns and the pastures, and Jack could see Suzy clearly, standing in the middle of the main pasture. Then he saw Monarch, the big Holstein bull, appear around the corner of the barn and begin to walk toward her. Horror-struck, the boy realized his father could never reach Suzy in time, for the vicious Monarch was in between, and the slightest irritation might make him charge at the little girl.

The bull stood watching Suzy, snorting nervously, slowly stabbing at the ground with his forefeet. At the gate, Mr. Miller shouted to Suzy to stop screaming and stand absolutely still, but the strong wind blew his words away and she could not hear him. Instead she continued to scream, and then she turned and began to run, the scarf on her head fluttering in the wind. The sight of the scarf made the bull begin to rumble with anger, and he backed off a few steps, still pawing the ground.

Suddenly, Suzy tripped and fell, sprawling on her face. She screamed again, and Monarch lowered his head with a mighty bellow. Then, like an avalanche of murderous fury, he charged.

Someone else had heard Monarch's angry bellow. At the sound of Suzy's first scream, Kata had looked up and stood listening, trying to make certain of the direction of the sound. Then he saw the bull come out from behind the barn and paw the ground. In the fraction of a second, the wolf dog acted. With one bound he launched himself off the porch, and plunged down the hill straight for the pasture fence.

Without stopping to go through the rails, the big wolf dog cleared the five-foot rails in a magnificent leap, and shot like a bolt of lightning toward the charging bull. Straight at Monarch's head he hurled himself, burying his razor fangs in the bull's sensitive nostrils.

The bull, now bellowing in pain, swung his mighty head into the air and tossed the big wolf dog twenty feet away as if he were a feather. Kata hit the ground with a thump, and the bull turned back to Suzy.

Once more Monarch lowered his head for a final charge. Again, out of nowhere, came the black and silver shadow, and this time the wolf dog changed his tactics. Now Kata instinctively fought as a wolf would fight; as his father, Red Fang, had many times attacked the giant bull moose, shifting in to slash and slash again, only to leap back quickly, out of reach of Monarch's wild lunges.

In his fury, the bull forgot Suzy and turned his full attention to this elusive enemy he could not reach. Time after time the bull charged, only to find the wolf dog not there. Each time Kata circled back again to rip and tear at the bull's nostrils, and each time the telling fangs left a smear of blood where they had gone deep.

Not for an instant did Kata let up his whirlwind attack, for his instinct also told him he was no match for the bull in sheer strength and size. This was a battle he could win only by his cunning.

For what seemed hours to those who were watching, the bull and the wolf dog fought there in the middle of the pasture. The battle seemed endless, but as it wore on the bull's wild rushes grew slower. After a time he stood, breathing heavily, his small red eyes warily watching his opponent. Still Kata could not slow his attack, for he must stay well out of reach of those terrible horns. One mistake, one misstep, and the wolf dog knew it would be all over.

Once, as Kata slipped on a patch of muddy ground, he twisted aside just in time to avoid the bull's charge. Then, out of the corner of his eye, Kata saw Suzy edging across the pasture toward the safety of the fence. Monarch saw her as well, and started forward, for a minute forgetting the wolf dog. But Kata would not let him forget. Again he leaped at the bull, snarling, slashing through hide and muscle to reach the tendon of the bull's hind legs, trying to hamstring him. The bull was too powerful, but Kata's ruse worked, for again Monarch turned back from the little girl to face this more immediate enemy.

But now Kata, too, was growing tired, and his constant rushes grew slower. Several times he barely escaped the bull's goring horns, but still he kept on, until at last he saw Suzy reach the safety of the fence, far over on the edge of the pasture.

Now the wolf dog's work was nearly done, but still he remembered his training. Like the cattle he herded every day, this massive bull, too, must be driven to the barn. Kata heard no signal from Jack, but his duty was clear.

Slowly, teasing the big bull just enough to insure his charging, the wolf dog began to work his way toward the barnyard. The bull was really tired now, and again he stopped for a moment and stood with lowered head. But Kata would not let him rest. Like a hornet the wolf dog flitted in to slash, and out again, backing off as the tired bull came after him. Now trotting ahead, now barking, he baited Monarch on.

In a few minutes they had reached the gates of the milkshed yard, and there Monarch halted, suspicious. Kata barked once, and barked again, standing right in front of the bull. Then he darted forward, and as Monarch lowered his horns, Kata shifted to the side and scuttled through the gates just ahead of the lunging bull.

In an instant Mr. Miller and Luke had slammed the gates shut, and Luke jumped in with the prodding stick. Quickly he cornered the tired bull and attached the stick to the ring in his nose, leading him into the barn.

Mr. Miller ran across the pasture to Suzy and brought the little girl back. She was crying from fear and shock, but she was not hurt. "Thanks to Kata," Mr. Miller said. "That dog has really proved his salt." He turned to Jack, who had run down from the house and was examining Kata carefully to see if the wolf dog had been gored by any passing swing of the bull's horns.

"Nope," the boy said. "Not a scratch. And, Suzy,"

turning to his sister, "next time you lose that kitten, you let Kata and me hunt for it!"

The little girl was happily fondling her kitten, which she had found in the pasture. Now she smiled at Jack. "Kata saved my kitty, didn't he, Jack?"

"He saved you, too, Suzy," Mr. Miller said gravely. "I want you to promise me never to go into the pasture alone again. You gave us all a scare today that we'll not forget for a long time."

"Yes, Daddy," Suzy said demurely.

They went up to the house to eat a delayed dinner, and tell the shaken Mrs. Miller that Suzy was perfectly all right. For a minute Jack held back with his wolf dog.

"Kata," the boy said, "I don't care if you don't even qualify in those shepherd-dog trials next week. After this, I *know* you're the best wolf dog in the world, winner or not."

Then the boy and the wolf dog followed the others up to the house.

Chapter 8

FRONTENAC CITY

URRY UP, Jack!" Mr. Miller called impatiently. The big wagon was all loaded with the family's suitcases, and they were all ready to leave. The boy had run back into the house at the last minute to hunt for Kata's brush, saying he wanted the wolf dog to look as well-groomed as the other dogs at the trials.

"What's taking that boy so long?" Mr. Miller grumbled, calling him again. This time Jack appeared, triumphantly waving the lost brush above his head.

"Found it!" he said breathlessly, climbing into the back seat of the wagon with Suzy and Kata. "It had fallen under the chest in the back hall, where Kata always hides it."

"Now we can go!" He grinned at his father. "The best cattle dog at the trials must be the best-looking, too!"

Mr. Miller chuckled. "Don't be too sure of winning yet, son," he said. "Remember, you'll be up against the stiffest competition in Canada, and Kata's not used to crowds of people."

Jack was not worried. He knew Kata would obey him down to the last hand signal, and that the wolf dog trusted him completely. "Even if he is scared by the people or the noise, he'll obey," the boy said confidently. "Besides, he knows his business about cattle herding, and once he gets started working those cows, he'll be too busy to be bothered."

Jack felt sure Kata could take the city in stride, too. "After all," he pointed out to his father, "with Kata's mother having been a German shepherd, even though he has a lot of Red Fang's wild strain in him, he's so smart he'll catch on in a hurry."

"Probably more quickly than you and Suzy!" smiled Mrs. Miller.

Mr. Miller planned to drive the wagon as far as Troutville, where he had made arrangements to have a truck driven up from Howardstown to meet them.

The long drive across the province to Frontenac City would take all day, even in a truck, and he wanted an early start.

The team set a good pace, however, and they soon covered the ten miles to Troutville, where the truck was waiting.

"Thanks, Lem," Mr. Miller said to the driver. "We'll be back in a few days. See you then."

"Glad to oblige, Bob. And good luck to you, Jack." Lem waved a cheerful hand as they drove off. He was an old friend of Mr. Miller's, and knew all about the plans to enter Kata in the trials. "Bring back a prize!" he called.

On the long drive, Jack and Suzy were too excited to sit quietly in the back of the truck. Jack constantly pointed out things of interest to Suzy, and he was as anxious to see everything as she was. Kata, too, peered out of the windows, watching. The children laughed at his reactions to some of the new sights, terribly pleased to have the big wolf dog along.

They drove steadily all morning along a dirt road, coming onto a paved highway just before lunch. The family stopped for lunch in a small town that had a teashop, but Jack and Suzy were so excited they could hardly eat, except for dessert. They both had big dishes of strawberry ice cream.

When they finished lunch Mr. Miller drove into

a gas station to fill the truck's tank, and he asked the proprietor how long it would take them to get to Frontenac City.

" 'Bout three hours," the man said. "What part of the city you going to?"

Mr. Miller told him where Jack's grandmother lived. The man told him that when they came to the outskirts of the city to branch off on a road to the right. "That'll lead you across the new bridge," he said. "Takes you through a lot of traffic on the other side, but it's shorter, for where you're going."

They thanked him and drove away. As the afternoon wore on they passed through more and more towns, and the countryside changed from thick forests to farmland.

"Looks like there're a lot more farms over here than in New Brunswick, Dad," commented Jack.

"That's right, son. We've left the backwoods now, where the country is wild. In this part of Canada the land is more settled, mostly with farms and lots of little towns. We'll stop at the next stretch of open country to let Kata out of the truck. It's the last real run he'll be able to have for several days. You'll have to keep him on a leash while we're at your grandmother's house. It's right in the middle of the city."

He stopped the truck on the side of the road by a big open field, and Jack took Kata out. The big wolf dog stretched and yawned after the hours of being confined, and bounded around, barking happily. Some birds flew up from underfoot and Kata ran along under them, then circled, and came panting back to Jack.

Mr. Miller honked the horn to signal them back to the truck. "Come on, fellow, we've got to get going," Jack told the dog. "You've had enough exercise for the time being."

Around five o'clock the highway came to a river, and turned to follow its banks. Far over on the other side, Jack and Suzy could see first the houses, and then more and more of the tall buildings rising high into the sky. "That's Frontenac City," Mr. Miller told them. "It won't be long now before we're there, after we cross the bridge."

He found the road the gas station man had told them about, leading onto the great bridge spanning the river. Jack noticed that Kata seemed restless, and began to move about the floor of the back seat, whining. "What do you suppose is the matter with him, Jack?" Suzy asked.

"Guess he's just tired of riding, aren't you, Kata? Here, boy, get up on the seat and you can stick your head out the window. Maybe that'll make you feel better."

"I do hope he's not getting carsick," Mrs. Miller said, turning around to look at Kata.

They started across the bridge, which rose in a

high arc over the river, and Jack and Suzy could see the city stretching out in front of them. Coming down the far side of the bridge, they passed through big stone gates. Beyond the gates the change was abrupt. Now they were right in the midst of the traffic, with automobiles seemingly whizzing in all directions, horns blaring, engines roaring.

"They look like they're going to hit us!" said Suzy, frightened by the busy streets.

"Don't worry, they won't." Mrs. Miller reassured her. "Kata's scared, too."

The wolf dog was whining, and becoming increasingly restless. He got down on the floor of the truck, and lay there panting.

"It's just all the noise and confusion," Mr. Miller said. "Leave him alone, and give him time to get used to it."

"Look, Suzy, there's a streetcar!" Jack pointed out the big vehicle, which came toward them along the tracks in the middle of the street.

"Will it stay on the tracks, Mother, and not hit us?" Suzy asked.

"Of course, silly," Jack said. He felt very superior to his sister, because he knew about streetcars. He had read of them in school. "It just makes a lot of noise, that's all."

When they drew alongside the streetcar its bell clanged loudly and Kata began to bark at the noise.

The big wolf dog could not see the streetcar from his place on the floor, and he did not understand all the noise. What was his master doing, bringing him in a rumbling, closed-in box to a place where huge animals roared at him? These animals were too big to fight!

Now Kata had only one desire, to be back on the farm. There he had the Great Woods to run in, and the only animals he saw were ones he knew how to fight. It was quiet and peaceful on the farm, and not like this place, which was beyond his understanding.

Here the wolf dog's native instinct was to lie low, and wait. He would stay on the floor patiently until Jack took him back to the farm, and opened the door of the truck. Then he would bound out into the front yard of the farmhouse, and run around in the trees and grass. He knew how to act there. Meanwhile, in this strange place where all was noise and new things, he would have to trust his master.

But, suddenly, Kata heard the clanging bell of the streetcar. This was too much! Confused though he was, he knew such a big animal was dangerous, and it was coming toward them, toward his master! He had to protect the boy, no matter how frightened he was himself.

As the streetcar slowly passed them, Kata hurled

himself toward the glass window, trying to attack the monster. The glass held, throwing him back, and he began to bark again. In the small space the raucous noise hurt the family's ears!

"What in the world will we do with him?" Mrs. Miller asked.

"I still say he'll be all right if you leave him alone," Mr. Miller answered. "You must give an animal like that time to get used to the city."

They drove as rapidly as possible along the crowded main thoroughfare of Frontenac City until they came to the cross boulevard where Jack's grandmother lived. Here Mr. Miller turned, and in a few short blocks the truck pulled up to the curb.

"Well, here we are," Mr. Miller said. "How's Kata now, Jack?"

The wolf dog had subsided onto the floor of the back seat after the streetcar had been left behind, and his outburst of barking quieted to whines.

"Hold tight to the leash," Mrs. Miller said, as they got out of the car, for Jack's grandmother lived on a street that was nearly as full of traffic as the main thoroughfare.

"Why, Grandmother doesn't even have a front yard!" Suzy exclaimed. "Where does she play?"

The house was right on the sidewalk, and after the family greetings were over, Jack asked his grandmother if there was any place he could take Kata to exercise. He wanted to try to get the wolf dog back to his old self.

"Unfortunately, no," said his grandmother. "There are no parks near here, but I do have a pocket-sized back garden. You can take him out there if you like."

She seemed a little afraid of Kata. "He's very big, isn't he? Didn't you tell me his father was a wolf, Jack? I don't know how a creature like that's going to get on in the city. You know the shepherd-dog trials are held in a big indoor ice skating rink, not out in the fields."

Jack was dismayed when he heard this news. He had entered Kata in the trials by mail, and had received no information from the trial authorities other than a schedule of judging and a number for Kata.

"Well, I guess Kata will be okay. At least there'll be the cattle for him to work with, and that's all he needs."

Jack took the wolf dog into the back yard, but it was so small the big animal had no room to run. He walked around on the end of the leash, sniffing the brick walkway, and seemed to be more uneasy than ever.

"You've got to hurry up and get used to the city, Kata," Jack said. "I know it's hard, but the trials are day after tomorrow, and you haven't got much time."

The big wolf dog looked up at the boy. Solemnly he stood up on his hind legs and put his forepaws on the boy's shoulders. He licked Jack's face. "I know, Kata," the boy said, "if you could talk you'd say you want to go home. I guess it was a mistake to bring you, but now we're here we've got to do our best in these trials."

His words were interrupted by Mrs. Miller, calling from the back door that it was time for supper. Jack took Kata in and tied his leash to the dining-room door while the family ate. After supper everybody went to bed early. The Millers were all tired from the long day's drive, and Jack wanted to get up early. Maybe tomorrow he could find out if there was a place big enough for Kata to run in.

In the morning Jack was awakened by Kata, who stood by the bed, poking his cold nose into the sleeping boy's face. He was whining, and when Jack got out of bed Kata began to walk around the room, as though he couldn't wait to be let out.

"I can't take you for a run yet, Kata," Jack said. "The nearest place for you to run is outside the city, and we can't drive you through all that traffic again."

The boy spent the morning sitting on the back steps with the wolf dog on a leash. Mr. and Mrs. Miller had taken Suzy sight-seeing around the city, but Jack didn't want to leave Kata.

The wolf dog was a little quieter, but he still seemed too uneasy for Jack's liking. Kata was all right as long as he could stay close to Jack, and the boy decided to stay with the wolf dog up until the time of the trials the next day. Every time the wolf dog heard the rumble of a big truck, or an auto horn blaring in the street, he growled, and tried to push himself between the noise and his master.

"Kata, I think you're trying to protect me from the city!" Jack smiled. "You'd face anything, wouldn't you? Even when you're afraid. That's real courage, fellow." Then he rumpled the big wolf dog's ears, until Kata quieted down again.

After lunch Jack's grandmother came in with a worried expression and said a friend had just telephoned.

"Her little daughter is very sick, Jack. I must go and see what I can do to help. I'm sorry to have to leave you, though. Will you be all right here, by yourself?"

"I'll be fine, Grandmother," Jack said, seeing how upset she was. "You go right ahead and don't worry about me. Besides, I'm not alone, with Kata."

She looked fearfully at the great wolf dog. "Well, then, I just hope he behaves . . ." she said, putting on her coat.

"He'll behave, Grandmother, don't worry."

After she had gone the boy settled himself in the living room and picked up a magazine. Kata lay at Jack's feet, ears pricked, alert for any new and unknown danger.

The boy read for more than an hour, until suddenly the silence of the house was broken by the doorbell.

"Wonder who that is?" Jack said to Kata. The wolf dog was on his feet, barking at the strange sound. "I think I'll tie you up before I answer, just to keep you from causing any trouble."

He looped Kata's leash loosely around the chair leg, and went into the front hall to answer the door. When he opened it, a man smiled politely and asked for Jack's grandmother.

"She's not here," the boy said. "She had to go out."

The man said she had telephoned him to come and fix a leak in the kitchen sink. "Well," Jack said, "my grandmother left in such a hurry she probably forgot about you, but I guess you can come in."

"It's all right," said the workman. "I know what's wrong with it; I only have to put in a new washer. Won't take a minute."

He stepped into the front hall and started to take off his coat. At that instant, a black and silver shape hurtled past Jack with an awful snarl, and launched himself at the workman's throat. The man staggered backward with a scream of terror, throwing out his arms to protect his face, as the wolf dog struck with all the full force of his ninety-five pounds.

"Kata, No! NO!" Jack shouted, but the wolf dog paid no attention. The strain of the past twenty-four hours had become too much for him, and he scarcely even heard the boy's voice. Quickly Jack grabbed the broken leash that still dangled from Kata's collar. He stepped backward and jerked the leash as hard as he could. "Kata, COME!" he shouted, and this time, through a red haze of hate in his brain, the wolf dog heard. For a minute he hesitated, and Jack jerked again. This time he quickly looped the free end of the leash around the front doorknob, and Kata, still growling, backed off from the prostrate workman.

Jack led the wolf dog into the living room and shut the door. When he came back into the hall, the workman was just getting to his feet. The blood was dripping from his arms.

"Your wolf has torn my arm to the bone!" he said angrily. "I'll sue you for this! He ought to be shot, or you ought to be, for having a vicious brute like that around!"

Jack offered to help the man wash off the blood, and bandage the ragged cuts from Kata's fangs, but the workman refused.

"You tell your grandmother that she'll be hearing from me, all right! Or from the police! Don't you know there's a law against keeping vicious dogs in this city?" With that, he walked through the front door and slammed it shut behind him.

"Whew!" Jack breathed, leaning weakly against the wall. "Now we're in for it—Kata and I. I wonder what Dad will say."

He went into the living room, pushing the still growling Kata away from the door. The wolf dog couldn't understand why Jack didn't pet him, the way the boy usually did when he had done something good. Hadn't he saved his master from an unknown danger? Kata had often barked violently whenever a strange trapper or hunter passed the farm on their way down-river, and no one ever had scolded him then. This was the same thing. Even though he was in a new place, he knew that no stranger had any business in the house.

Now, instead of praising him, the boy was just standing there. "You shouldn't have done that, Kata," Jack said. "You've got us in trouble, in a big way. I know you didn't understand that man was harmless, but you didn't obey me when I called you the first time. But then," he said, stooping down and putting his arms around the dog at last, "you did come the second time, and you thought you were protecting me, didn't you? Only," he looked thoughtful, "what am I going to tell Dad?"

And the police, and my grandmother, the boy thought. Boy, Kata's really got things in a mess.

Just then the front door opened and Mr. and Mrs. Miller and Suzy walked in. Jack could hear them talking gaily in the hall, discussing their day of sightseeing. He left Kata and went to tell his father what had happened.

Mr. Miller looked grave. "This is pretty serious, Jack. I only hope it's not as bad as it sounds. Who was this workman?" he asked. "The first thing to do is get in touch with him and offer to pay his doctor's bill. Then perhaps he won't cause too much trouble."

"I don't know," Jack said. "But we can find out when Grandmother comes home."

In a few minutes she too arrived, and her face darkened when she heard the news of Kata's attack. "I just knew that wolf was going to cause trouble, the minute I saw him," she said. "You can't have an animal like that with so much bad blood in him, and not expect him to turn wild. Sooner or later they all do."

Jack opened his mouth to protest, but his father motioned him to be quiet. There was no point in upsetting his grandmother any more.

"The important thing is to get hold of that workman and offer to pay his doctor's bill," Mr. Miller repeated. "Do you know who he was?"

"Yes," said Grandmother. "I can do that much anyway. I'll get him on the telephone."

She came back from the phone looking more worried than ever. "He's terribly upset, but he won't sue us if we promise to pay all his doctor's bill. He's already called the police. He says Kata is so vicious he ought to be shot, and, frankly, I'm inclined to agree with him. I'm sorry, Bob," she said to Mr. Miller, "but that's just the way I feel. I declare it makes me nervous, having that wolf in my house."

Mr. Miller said they would take Kata home just as soon as the trials were over. In the meantime, Jack could keep him in the basement. "He can't get near anyone down there, and we don't want him to bite the police."

The police! What would they do with Kata? Quickly Jack took the wolf dog down to the cellar, hoping the police wouldn't ask to see him. By the time the boy came back up the cellar steps, two policemen were standing in the front hall, talking to his father. "Oh, here you are, Jack," said Mr. Miller. "You'd better tell these officers exactly what happened."

"Sure, Dad, but it was just like I told you. Kata isn't used to the city, officer," the boy said, addressing himself to the police sergeant. "He thought that workman was going to hurt me, and he wanted to protect me, the way he's used to doing on the farm."

"I'm not interested in this wolf's reasons," said the sergeant. "I'm only concerned that he bit a man, very badly, and we have a law here in Frontenac City that no one is allowed to keep a vicious dog. Where is he now?"

Jack explained that Kata was in the basement, and held his breath. What would they do?

But the sergeant only nodded curtly. "Well," he said, "you keep him there until you go back to the farm. Your father tells me you've entered him in the shepherd-dog trials, but that's out of the question, now. That wolf will have to stay muzzled and in the cellar until you leave here. Otherwise, if he gets into any more trouble, we'll have to shoot him."

Shoot him? Shoot Kata? "Oh, no, officer," Jack begged. "Please, he's a good dog. I won't let him out any more."

"See to it that you don't," the officer said. Turning to Mr. Miller, he suggested they take Kata home at once. "We have our laws, and if you want to keep the wolf, you'll have to take him back where he belongs. He certainly doesn't belong in a city."

Jack stood watching as the policemen climbed into their car and drove away. Kata couldn't enter the shepherd-dog trials! "Oh, Dad," the boy said, "after all that training. I know he would have won!"

"Well, son, it is too bad. But frankly, we're lucky

I don't have a lawsuit on my hands, and that the sergeant let Kata off as easily as he did. With their laws here, he might very well have been shot. You're lucky the sergeant just told you to take him home."

Jack turned sadly away. Kata's big chance was gone, his chance to prove he could be trusted, as a cattle dog, or as a pet.

"But *I* know he can be trusted," Jack muttered to himself. "I haven't forgotten how he rescued Luke and me, and saved Suzy. Someday, somehow, I'll make Dad believe in him too!"

That night when Jack took Kata his food, the big wolf dog could sense something was wrong. He jumped up on the boy and tried to lick his face, and Jack scratched his ears.

"It's my fault, Kata," the boy said. "I should have tied the leash tighter. Now I have to leave you down here, because of what that sergeant said. But don't you mind, old fellow; tomorrow we're going home, and you'll be happy again." He took off Kata's muzzle so the wolf dog could eat, and then he went up the cellar steps and closed the door firmly behind him.

Left alone, the wolf dog only sniffed at his food. He could still hear the rumbling of the huge city all about him, and it made him too uneasy to eat. Where was the call of the night owl, or the bark of a fox, or the sound of the cows lowing in the pasture? This land was foreign, and Kata did not like it.

He made a circuit of the cellar, standing on his hind legs to peer out of a small grilled window, but there was no exit. He went over and curled up in a corner to wait for morning, when his master would come and get him. Maybe he could run loose then.

That night the wolf dog slept fitfully. In his dreams he was far away, running over the snowy wastes with a wolf pack that was strange to him, and yet at the same time he seemed to belong with them. Kata's paws twitched, and from time to time he whined. He dreamed that the leader of the pack, a huge gray timber wolf, stood on a knoll high above the fir forests. The gray wolf was howling, calling his pack to the chase. In Kata's dream the eerie voice echoed across valley and hill, and when Kata woke in the musty cellar, he did not know where he was for a minute.

Then he remembered, for all around him was the smell of soot and dirt, the smell of the city, and the wolf dog's nose wrinkled into a snarl.

He got up and threw back his head, and there, in the musty cellar, as he had by the pool in the forest, he answered the gray wolf's call. A long-drawn-out howl, the howl of the wolf pack!

Upstairs, Jack woke up not knowing what he had

heard. For a minute he wondered sleepily if he had really heard a wolf howling, and then he rolled over in the covers again. "Must have been dreaming," he mumbled sleepily as he dozed off.

In the morning the Millers left Frontenac City. This time Jack and Suzy, on the back seat, were quiet, their spirits dampened. Jack felt almost despair, for Kata seemed to have changed overnight. The wolf dog was still affectionate, but at the same time he was distant, as if his mind were far away.

Mr. Miller left the city by a back route in order to avoid the heavy traffic, and the wolf dog lay quietly on the floor, scarcely raising his head. When Jack spoke to him, Kata looked up, but did not move.

"He seems to have resigned himself to the city," Mr. Miller said. "Fine time, now that we're leaving."

"I don't think that's it, Dad. I think there's more to it. Kata seems to have changed."

"Maybe he's really growing up," said Mrs. Miller.

If he is growing up, Jack wondered, will it be into a dog, or a timber wolf?

Chapter 9

KATA'S TRIAL

AUTUMN drew near. It was now the last of August, and soon school would begin. Jack made the most of the remaining summer days, taking off as much time as he could from his chores to roam the woods and fields with Kata.

The big wolf dog had seemed to become his old self almost as soon as he got back to the farm, but he was nearly full-grown now, and Jack could notice subtle changes in the wolf dog's character. Kata weighed close to one hundred pounds, with tremendous bone and muscle, and was a very powerful animal. The combined blood of his mother and father had produced an offspring bigger than either of them. He had his mother's coloring, with the jet-black coat and silver legs and muzzle and the dark-brown eyes of a German shepherd. From his father came the giant chest and depth of rib, and the huge size.

"How do the two combine inside of you, Kata?" Jack voiced his thoughts aloud one day, sitting under a tree where he and Kata had stopped to rest. They had explored a new stretch of woods near Trout-ville, and had been out all day. Now they were on their way home. Kata was lying at Jack's feet with his head on his paws, but his eyes seemed to be seeing something very far away. Was it the wolf pack? Jack wondered, or was it a picture of the German shepherd, quietly herding sheep, the trusted companion of the man he worshiped?

Jack shook his head impatiently. This was no way to think, not about Kata! Kata, who had rescued him and Luke, and saved Suzy from the bull. Where is my loyalty, the boy thought, the kind of loyalty that Kata has always shown to me? But still, the idea persisted in the back of Jack's mind that the big wolf dog was undergoing a great inward struggle. Not one the boy could see, but one he could sense was there.

Jack had noticed something odd that very afternoon, when they were walking quietly through a stand of spruce. A fox had sprung from his bed under a juniper bush, and Jack had whooped with excitement. "Go get him, Kata!" he shouted, knowing the wolf dog could never catch the clever Reynard.

Kata tore off after the fox, and the sounds of the chase receded into the distance. Jack climbed a little hill nearby, where he could get a better view. He knew the fox would soon circle, preferring to stay in known territory, the better to elude his barking pursuer.

Shading his eyes from the sun, Jack soon caught a glimpse of Kata, winded now. He was trotting slowly along, nose to the ground, and, as Jack had thought, the trail was leading back toward the boy in a wide circle. "That fox is probably miles away by now," Jack chuckled, "walking down the middle of some stream bed to drown his scent."

"Oh, well," he said, feeling disloyal to Kata. "Wolves aren't supposed to know how to hunt foxes, anyway; hounds do that! Give Kata a deer or a moose and it'd be a different story!"

Soon Kata was close by, but Jack still watched. He waited to see how the wolf dog followed the trail. Then the boy noticed that Kata was no longer following the trail; instead he had stopped in the middle of a small clearing. The wolf dog walked over to a little stream to drink, and then prowled through the clearing, sniffing the air. His ears were up, and he was looking toward the north.

Suddenly, a flock of wild geese flew overhead, fleeing southward from the coming winter, and their honking filled the sky with music. The big wolf dog heard them, too, and looked up. They seemed to make up his mind, for without any more hesitation he turned his face in the opposite direction, and started at a steady lope toward the north.

Without stopping to think, Jack ran forward, and shouted. "Kata, Kata, come back!" Jack called. The wolf dog paused in mid-stride, faltered, and came to a standstill.

"Here, Kata. Here, boy," Jack called again. Still the wolf dog didn't move, but when Jack called him for the third time, Kata turned around, and trotted slowly back to the boy.

"Good fellow, Kata. You know it's too late in the day to go tearing off like that!" Jack petted him.

But now, on their way home, sitting with his back against the tree, Jack thought more about the episode of the afternoon. Where had Kata been going, he wondered, and why did he head north, away from the farm? Would he have come back, the boy thought, if I hadn't called him?

"Well anyway," he said aloud to the dog, "I did call you, and I'm glad you came. We'll always stick together, won't we?" The wolf dog licked his hand. He seemed to have completely forgotten the fox hunt, lying peacefully now at Jack's feet.

A few days later Jack was talking to Luke down at the barn. They had finished the milking, and were leaning against the fence, enjoying the early autumn sunshine. Kata was with them, his dark-brown eyes fixed attentively as usual on Jack's face, watching the boy adoringly.

Luke had just come back from Troutville, where he had gone to pick up the mail and the weekly newspaper that was sent up from Howardstown. The hired man's leg was completely healed now, and, except for a slight stiffness which would disappear with time, he was as good as new.

Luke was as disappointed as Jack that Kata had been unable to compete in the shepherd-dog trials, but, as the hired man said, "The thing was, you didn't give him enough chance to get used to the city. Dog like that has to have time to get used to new surroundings, like any animal that's only been in the backwoods."

"Yes," Jack agreed. "Maybe if we hadn't gone that short way to my grandmother's house, and sprung that traffic on him all of a sudden, he wouldn't have acted the way he did.

"He seemed better when we left, too," the boy

continued. "Only it was too late then, for this year's trials, anyway."

"Well, there'll always be another time," Luke smiled. "Keep on working him with the cattle, and maybe your father'll let you try again next year. Speaking of Frontenac City, I saw in the paper where a convict named Bart escaped from the big penitentiary there. A half-breed murderer, the paper said. Tied up a trapper and stole his fur cache, then left him to starve. Even gagged him so he couldn't lick the snow for water. Then the breed figured maybe someone'd find the trapper and get his description, so he came back and this time he tied the trapper to a tree. He slashed him to death with a hunting knife, like he was quartering a calf. The Mounties caught up with him, but he killed two of them and wounded another. Now he's escaped, got clean away. They think maybe he's heading over this way, into New Brunswick. Sure hope he stays away from here."

"Me, too," Jack sighed, looking at Kata and scarcely listening. "We've had enough trouble already."

"Just like Kata, got the law after him," Luke laughed heartily, and Jack tried to join in. The disappointment about the shepherd-dog trials still rankled in the boy; more than that, he felt the wolf dog was still in disgrace. That was the worst part.

Mr. Miller never said anything about it, but Jack noticed that whenever he started to tell his father about something good Kata had done, his father changed the subject.

Mr. Miller did not say anything more to Jack than he already had, but his doubts about the wolf dog, stilled by Kata's earlier feats, had now begun to reappear. Those acts had been performed while the wolf dog was still almost a puppy, but now he was growing into a huge animal, capable of anything. Who could tell what he might do?

But Mr. Miller held silent. The problem would solve itself, he felt, with the coming of winter. For winter would bring the wolf packs, and then they would see what happened.

In the meantime, Jack was busy helping with the fall chores of the farm, for there was much to be done to prepare for the winter. Soon the screaming winds of the blizzards would sweep out of the north, and the barn walls had to be well banked with earth to keep out the penetrating cold. The cows would be safely quartered inside, but they had to be fed, and the men spent many hours stacking the hay snugly in the lofts, to serve as food throughout the winter.

Shovels were brought out, and any flaw repaired. Soon they would be needed to dig paths through the snow to the watering troughs, or to clear the yards around the milk sheds. There must be an open space for the cows to go outside during the middle of the day and get fresh air, even in the worst of the winter weather.

At night the family and the hired men spent their time in a big room behind the kitchen, cleaning and repairing the snowshoes and the skis. Jack's school would open in two weeks, and he would have to make the ten-mile trek to Troutville every day on his snowshoes. The skis were for the men to use on any longer trips they might make into the backwoods. Out in the open where the going was hilly they could travel faster on skis than on the snowshoes, but in the forests, the snow was powdery and soft. There only the great webbed snowshoes, shaped like huge tennis rackets, would stay on top of the surface.

The sledges, too, were brought out after a summer's disuse and carefully scraped down. They were very necessary for hauling wood, and for carrying the milk pails. In the summer the men carried the heavy pails on yokes over their shoulders, but in winter the weight of the heavy pails made them flounder helplessly in the soft snow. This was when the sledges came into use, for even loaded with heavy pails of milk they slid easily over the surface.

Guns were brought out and oiled, for winter brought the big marauders, the wolves and the lynxes, and even the wolverine and the cougar. Becoming more and more desperate for food as the winter grew more severe, these kindred of the wild prowled close to the farm. Late at night they glided from the blackness of the fir forests, close up toward the barns, to raid the chicken house or even break into the calfpens.

Once a cougar had killed a young heifer, and Mr. Miller, roused by her death bellows, had surprised the big cat in the barn, crouched over its fresh kill. With a snarl the cougar had bounded up into the loft and out of a window, disappearing in the snow.

Mr. Miller had gone after it, but soon lost the track, and the cougar got away. He was one of the biggest Mr. Miller had ever seen, and when two days later a trapper shot one about a mile from the farm, he decided it was probably the same one. He was right, for they were no longer disturbed by that menace, but afterward Mr. Miller had double checked all the barn doors and windows to make sure they were tight.

Now there was something new to do each day, and always the wolf dog followed close at Jack's heels. He knew something was in the air, and he too felt a change in the atmosphere. At times the strange restlessness again came upon him, especially in the first crisp autumn nights, when the wind whined around the corners of the farmhouse. Then Kata would get up from his rug at the foot of Jack's bed, and walk slowly to the window, where he would rest his great muzzle on the sill and look out at the silent forests beyond the pasture.

The wolf dog did not know that it was the time of the coming together of the wolf pack in the Far North, after a summer of going their separate ways. He did not know that on these frosty nights the great Red Fang howled night after night to the arctic moon, calling his green-eyed running companions to be off after the big game. Kata felt only a faint stirring in the hairs along the back of his neck, for he heard nothing except the sounds of the farm, or the distant hoot of an owl.

Often he would leave the window and go over to Jack's bed, waking the boy up with a pushing nose, and whine, and lick Jack's face. "What is it, Kata?" Jack said. He petted the wolf dog and talked to him, until Kata was soothed into lying down again, and the restlessness was stilled for a time.

Only Jack knew of these spells of Kata's, and he said nothing to his family. He hoped the wolf dog would come out of it when the stirring of autumn stopped, and the heavy winter closed down on the countryside.

A week before school was due to begin, Jack was eating breakfast one morning when Luke appeared in the kitchen doorway. "Black-Crow's canoe is at the boat landing," he said. "He's coming up to the house."

"Oh, boy!" Jack shouted, rushing off and leaving his breakfast. "Come on, Kata! Black-Crow is back! I've sure missed him!"

The Indian looked the same as ever, and smiled when he saw Jack and Kata bounding beside him.

"He recognizes you, Black-Crow!" Jack exclaimed.

"And well he should. Would you have my prize of the trap forget Black-Crow in one short summer?" chuckled the Indian. He greeted the Millers and Luke, and then turned again to Jack.

"Your wolf dog has turned from a puppy into a king among dogs," he said. "And does he still live up to his name, the Wise One?"

There was a silence for a minute, and then Mr. Miller told the Indian a little bit about the trip to Frontenac City. When that unpleasant story was over, he told him, too, about the trip Kata had made from the cypress swamp for help, and about Suzy and the bull.

"He is truly a combination of his mother, the German shepherd, and of his father Red Fang, the great leader of the wolf pack."

"Yes," said Mr. Miller, "and I'm only hoping that his mother's blood is the stronger!"

Black-Crow walked over to Kata and put his hand on the wolf dog's head. For a long minute the Indian looked into his eyes, and Kata met the gaze with his own steady dark-brown ones. The wolf dog did not flinch for an instant.

Then Black-Crow looked up at the Millers. He gave Kata a friendly pat, and said, "This Kata, the Wise One, is no wolf. He has the blood of Red Fang in him, it is true, but only the best of what that blood can give him. He has his father's cunning, his father's great strength, and his father's great spirit. But that is all. I have looked into his eyes, and I have seen his mother's heart."

Then the Indian walked up to the house, and sat down to breakfast with Mr. and Mrs. Miller. Jack's food was cold. "I'll get you some more," his mother smiled, "since it's a special occasion."

Black-Crow sat for some time at the breakfast table, telling them about his summer in the cabin at the headwaters of the Mamozekel. He had had good hunting, he said, and had gotten many fish to bait his traps in the winter.

"Speaking of traps, Black-Crow," Mr. Miller said, "yours are all safely cached where Jack and Luke put them for you. But isn't it a little early to start your trap line? We've had no snow yet, and you don't usually set your line before the snows are well started. What changed your mind this year?"

"It is not the trap line that I have come for, Mr. Miller, though I will stay on and set it out in a few weeks' time. It is the hunt for the man. I want to help, because I want no renegades loose far up in the bush, when I am there alone this winter! Look at the trouble caused by the renegade poacher who reset my bear trap in the cypress swamp."

"What man?" asked Mr. Miller, bewildered.

"Guess it's my fault," interrupted Luke. "Completely slipped my mind the other day. Forgot to tell you about the escaped convict. They saw him in Howardstown, and he came on up the river. Hid out in the bush somewheres near that old mining town about twenty miles beyond Troutville. Mounties are after him, but no luck so far."

"That is right," Black-Crow said. "The constable has asked us all to join in the search. He sent word to me, up the Mamozekel, to keep watch, and that is why I have come so early. Winter is bad enough in our country without vicious outlaws also."

"Well," said Mr. Miller, "I'm glad to hear about it now, anyway. We can take the wagon and drive into Troutville right now, and find out if they've had any luck. Give you a lift, too, Black-Crow."

Luke went down to the barn to hitch up the team, while Mr. Miller and Black-Crow waited in the front yard. They discussed the possibilities of the convict's whereabouts.

When Jack could break in, he asked his father if he could ride into Troutville with them.

"Yes, but you'll have to leave Kata behind. We're in a hurry, and we haven't got time to keep an eye on him. Shut him up in the barn, and do it quickly."

Kata barked anxiously when Jack put him in one of the old box stalls. The wolf dog hated to be separated from Jack for even a moment, and he hated even more being confined in a small space. "You'll have to stay there till I get back, Kata. I won't be long," Jack said consolingly.

The wolf dog seemed to accept his words, and settled himself in some straw bales in the corner. Jack ran out and climbed on the wagon, and Luke picked up the reins.

"Now we'll see what all this is about," Mr. Miller said.

When they got to Troutville, Luke drove straight to the constable's office. A crowd of men was gathered in front, and they were all carrying guns. Jack's father saw a friend and asked him the news.

"The convict's holed up somewhere. At least we think he's holed up in one of the old mines 'round that ghost town upriver. Constable McTavish's been combing the place for two days now, so it don't look too good. He may have gone off into the bush. Somebody found an old piece of cloth in a campsite and they think it's the cuff off his convict's uniform."

"That is quite possible," muttered Black-Crow. "I must go. The constable will need every tracker."

The other men continued to talk, but Jack's brain was filled with sudden inspiration. Trackers! That's what Black-Crow had said! And that meant some-one, probably one of the Indian trappers, who was good at finding a man's trail. The Indians could tell by every blade of grass bent down, and every leaf turned a wrong way, which direction a man had gone.

But, Jack knew, the constable had been searching for several days now, and the trail was cold. Even an Indian couldn't follow a very cold trail, Jack thought to himself. But a dog. A good trailing dog could follow any trail, as long as his nose held out. And that meant Kata.

Kata could follow that trail, Jack knew! If, and it was a big if, he could persuade his father to let him try the wolf dog!

Just then he realized the men were leaving. Some were loading their packs before starting toward the mining town, and others were going back to their homes to get guns and equipment. Constable McTav-ish had asked all available men in the district to help him, and nearly all had responded.

"You go on, Black-Crow," Mr. Miller said. "Luke and I'll go back to the farm and get our camp packs, and follow as soon as we can." The Indian nodded, and with a wave of farewell strode off up the trail toward the mining town.

On the trip back, Jack debated how to bring up his plan of using Kata. He was pretty sure his father wouldn't agree at first, and he wanted to have all his arguments ready.

Mr. Miller and Luke were discussing the places the man might be hiding, and when they mentioned the torn cuff, Jack found his opening. "Dad," he said, "will you let me take Kata up there with you? I'll keep him on a leash all the time," the boy rushed on before his father could say anything, "and I know he can follow that trail. It's too old by now for any of the men to do it, because the grass doesn't stay down but a few hours. Even the tree branches come back into place in a day. But Kata can use his nose and follow the trail just the way I taught him to do when the cattle are lost. Please, Dad, let me try. I want him to have a chance to prove he's not a bad dog, after what happened in Frontenac City. Please, Dad. I promise not to let him off the leash."

Mr. Miller looked at the boy. "I don't think so, Jack. How would Kata know what to look for? This is a man we're after, a killer. He's not a cow."

"I know, Dad, but there's that piece of cloth, the cuff they found. I heard you say the constable hadn't let anyone touch it, so the scent's still on it. I can let Kata sniff that, and tell him 'go find' the way I always do when I want him to track. I'm sure he can do it, Dad."

"Well," Mr. Miller said thoughtfully, "it's not such a bad idea, at that. What do you think, Luke?"

"Kata's a right smart cattle dog, Mr. Miller. I think he might be able to do it, if Jack can get the idea across. But what's going to happen if he *can* follow the trail and he catches up with the convict? They say the fellow's armed, and even if he didn't shoot Kata, which he probably would, Kata would tear him up some, way he did that workman. Constable wouldn't like that."

"That's right, Jack," Mr. Miller said. "You'd have to be very careful to keep Kata under control, and stay back once he finds the man. Bart's got a gun, and I don't want you anywhere around when he starts shooting."

"I'm sure Kata wouldn't even want to bite Bart, Dad," Jack said earnestly. "This would be just a job to him, like finding something I tell him to. He could just bark until the men can capture Bart, and I'll stay out of range. This is his chance, Dad. Please let him take it!"

Mr. Miller was silent for a while, while he thought what to do. "All right, Jack, it's worth a try. But I must tell you in all fairness that if Kata attacks anyone, and if he doesn't behave, you will have to get rid of him. He's done some wonderful things, but he also muffed his chance in Frontenac City. This will have to be the last time he gets another."

Chapter 10

MAN HUNT

BY LUNCHTIME they were ready, and in spite of Mrs. Miller's protests, the three of them decided to take sandwiches instead of wasting time eating at the farm.

"You've got a long trip ahead of you," Mrs. Miller said. "You need a good hot meal."

"We'll have to save it till we get back this time, Mary," Mr. Miller said. "Now don't worry; I'll see to it that Jack doesn't get hurt, and we'll be back as soon as we can."

"Good luck," she called to them from the doorway.

At Troutville they had to leave the horses and the wagon, for the trail beyond was too narrow for even a cart. They walked in single file, Mr. Miller first, then Luke, with Jack and Kata bringing up the rear. Kata was on the leash, as Jack had promised. The wolf dog pulled at first, not understanding why he couldn't run free as he usually did when he and Jack walked in the woods.

"We've got a long way to go, Kata, and besides you're on trial this time," the boy whispered, "so try to understand, and behave!"

The words quieted the wolf dog, and after that he walked sedately at Jack's heels.

Late in the afternoon they ate a quick supper of the food left over from lunch, and with the aid of a flashlight kept on after dark. The trail was narrow, but it was well-marked, and, as Mr. Miller said, "We're in a hurry. The constable needs every man he can get up there, fast!"

Around eleven o'clock they came to a clearing, and here they built a small fire to keep off the autumn chill and quickly rolled up in their blankets. Almost at once they were asleep, and when Luke wakened Jack at dawn, the boy felt as though he had only been asleep for a few minutes. "Boy, did I sleep like a log!" he exclaimed. He let Kata run for a few minutes while they ate breakfast, and then put the wolf dog back on the leash. Soon they broke camp and started off again.

By noon they had arrived at the mining town, where they found Constable McTavish in what had once been an old bank. He was talking to part of his posse. Many years before, this had been a thriving place, but the iron-ore deposits had petered out after a time. Now the once-bustling town was an empty shell.

When the constable saw Mr. Miller he greeted him enthusiastically. "Glad to see you here, Miller. We've got quite a job on our hands. One of the men found a two-day-old campsite about three miles north of here. That means our man has given us the slip. He must be headed toward the mountains, and if he gets there before we catch up he'll lose us in that trackless wilderness."

Black-Crow appeared out of the crowd and came over. "I have followed his trail as far as I can, but he took to the stream. It will take me too long to search both banks to find the place where he came out. I need more trackers, Constable."

McTavish shook his head. "You're the best of them, Black-Crow, and the others say the trail is too old to follow now. We'll just have to head for the mountains, and if we spread out one of us may come across something. As far as we know Bart's only got a rifle—no real camping equipment—so that'll be some help. He'll have to go slower than we do anyway. He's not sure of his ground."

"Still doesn't look good, not one bit," one of the men muttered.

Jack stepped forward and waited until the constable had finished speaking to one of his deputies. Then he led Kata up to McTavish, but before the boy could begin, the man said, "What's that you've got there? Looks like a wolf!"

"No, sir, he's not. His mother was a shepherd dog, and he's the best cattle dog you ever saw. I think he can find your man for you, and quick, too, if you'll give him a chance."

The constable shook his head. "I don't care what his mother was, he looks like a wolf to me. I can't risk turning an animal like that loose after Bart. I've told the commissioner in Frontenac City we'll bring this fellow back in one piece, and from the looks of your pet, there, not much'd be left of Bart after he got through with him. We'll just stick to my original plan, and let the Indians keep trying to find the trail."

Mr. Miller stepped forward. "McTavish, I can vouch for the dog. I think you ought to let him have a try at picking up the trail, anyway. Then you can decide what you want to do about following it. Kata's just about the best tracking dog I've ever seen, and I'm inclined to think he'll find Bart for you. We haven't got much time, you know."

The constable hesitated. He looked at Kata, standing quietly on his leash, and at Jack. Then he turned to Mr. Miller. "Well, Bob, you ought to know cattle dogs, if anybody does. If you say this wolf can track, I'll take your word for it. And you're right, we've got to find that trail in a hurry. We'll give him a try," he said, turning to Jack. "But mind you keep him tight on that leash."

"Yes, sir, Constable, I will," Jack promised. "Thanks, Dad," the boy said, as the constable strode off. "I didn't know you'd stick up for Kata like that."

"I told you I'd give him one more chance," Mr. Miller smiled.

In a few minutes they were ready to leave. The men picked up their equipment, ready to go, but the constable stopped them. "No," he said, "I'll go up the stream with the boy myself, while he works the dog. Too many of you with us might confuse him. When, and if, we pick up the trail, I'll fire two shots, to signal you to come on. We'll wait for you where we are."

One of the men brought up the torn cuff of Bart's convict uniform. It was wrapped in a piece of paper, to keep the scent intact. Jack held the paper out in front of Kata, for the wolf dog to see. Kata sniffed it, and then lost interest, turning away. Jack put the wolf dog's nose on it again. "Go find, Kata, go find," he repeated, and Kata seemed to understand. He sniffed the cuff again, more carefully this time. The boy pointed to the ground and obediently Kata put his nose down and began to walk in wide circles, Jack following. But then he stopped and sat down, whining.

"He will find nothing here," Black-Crow said. "The men have been walking around all morning and the scent is lost. We must take him to Bart's campsite. There will be much scent, for I disturbed nothing."

"You better come with us too, Black-Crow," the constable said. "You other men, remember, listen for our rifle shots."

As they came up to the campsite Kata began to whine again, this time in an excited manner.

"He has gotten Bart's scent," Black-Crow said. "Let him circle now, until he picks up the trail leading away from the camp."

Kata made two false starts on trails that ended at a nearby spring, but suddenly he began to pull hard on the leash, and started northward at a brisk pace.

"That's good," the constable said. "He's heading straight for the stream. Now to see what he'll do when he finds Bart's taken to the water."

At the bank of the stream, a mile farther on, Kata

came to an abrupt halt. He walked out into the
water a little way, and then came back to the bank,
starting up one side of the stream. "We'll let him
try this side first," McTavish said. "Seems as though
he knows what he's doing."

But by nightfall they had gone ten miles, and still
Kata had not hit any trail where Bart had come out
of the water. Every foot of the way had been tested
by the wolf dog's keen nose, but it was obvious that
he was only testing, not really on a trail.

That night Jack and the two men wearily rolled
up in their blankets, and were almost instantly
asleep. Kata lay down with a sigh of exhaustion. The
day had been a gruelling one for him as well.

In the morning, Jack suggested that instead of
going back to yesterday's starting point, they should
cross over right where they were. They could try to
pick up the trail on the opposite side, working further up the stream.

"All right," said Constable McTavish. "Bart's a
desperate man, and he probably kept to the water
for at least 15 or 20 miles, or so. We'll just take a
chance that he didn't get out below here, and head
off into the bush."

They crossed with little difficulty, and once again
Jack gave Kata the cuff to sniff. He wanted the wolf
dog's memory to be constantly refreshed.

Kata was sure, now, what his master wanted.

After the night's rest he started out with renewed energy, quartering the ground in circles for nearly three-quarters of an hour.

The going got rougher and rougher, through matted underbrush and impenetrable thorn thickets growing by the edge of the water. The men had to take precious time to work around bad places that Kata, loose, could have slithered through in seconds. But the constable did not suggest unleashing Kata, and Jack said nothing. He knew the wolf dog could have worked far better running free, but he had made a promise and he would keep it.

Finally McTavish called a halt. "Maybe we'd better go back downstream again, and try below where we started this morning. We aren't having much luck up here, unless the dog hasn't really been trying."

"He tries, Constable McTavish," said Black-Crow, "of that I am sure. I have been keeping a careful watch, and myself have seen no signs of a man's passing through here. Let us go on for another hour, and if he finds nothing by then, we will turn back."

"What do you say, Jack?" McTavish asked.

"I say go on, sir," said the tired boy. "Kata knows what he's hunting for, and you said yourself Bart might have stayed in the stream for as much as twenty miles. He wanted to go north, and now the stream's swinging west, so this is the side he'll have to come out on. I side with Black-Crow; give Kata another hour."

The constable agreed, and they went on. The stream began to run through heavy forests of pine and fir, and the ground opened out to a smooth, needle-covered floor under the great trees. They made good time, and Kata worked steadily. Ahead a patch of reeds poked out into the stream. The men were about to swing inland to get around it, when suddenly Kata barked once, sharply.

The wolf dog stopped, and carefully circled a small area of ground on the outskirts of the reeds. Then, with another bark, he turned and, head down, tugged hard on the leash, straining toward the forest.

"He's found it!" Jack cried.

"Yes, the boy is right," said the Indian tersely. "See, here the reeds are still bent down—only a little bit after two days, but the trail is there."

"What shall we do now, sir?" Jack asked the constable.

"I don't know. We're too far away for the men to hear my rifle signals, and it would waste too much time to go back. If we go ahead we've got a chance of getting Bart even with the lead he has. He probably thinks we're still looking for him back at the mining town and is taking his time."

"Oh, sir, let's go on," begged Jack. "Kata can follow the trail easily now, and if we don't go back the men will probably get worried and come after us anyway."

"Yes," said Black-Crow, "we can leave markers here for them to find, and blaze our trail as we go. I, too, think that we should go on. We have our guns, Constable, and that is all we need."

McTavish nodded assent. Jack let Kata drink from the stream, and then the boy took a firm hold on the leash and pointed into the fir trees. "Go find, Kata," he said.

By late afternoon they came out of the heavily forested country into a little valley that ran between two ridges. They decided to camp there for the night. While Jack and the constable unrolled the packs, Black-Crow went off to see what lay beyond the far ridge.

He came back to report that he had sighted the mountains, far to the north. "That means we've got to travel even faster tomorrow," the constable said.

They were up two hours before dawn, and after gulping down a hasty breakfast of tea and bannock, they broke camp and headed over the ridge. As the sun rose they were well into the next valley. Beyond that were no more ridges, but the country began to rise steadily, and they could see the blue outlines of the mountains more clearly.

Kata kept on steadily. Now his nose was down, testing each inch of ground when the trail grew faint over rocks or bare patches; now going fast over spongy turf, head up, where the scent was strong and his sensitive nose could pick out Bart's track from the labyrinth of game trails.

The wind rose, blowing from the west, and at times Kata worked ten yards east of the trail, for the scent blew with the wind. The big wolf dog was sure now of what Jack wanted, and kept to his job with a tenacity inherited from his mother and from Red Fang.

At noon the little group stopped to eat and give Kata a rest. The wolf dog's nose smarted, for he was working so close to the ground that the wind constantly blew small particles of dirt and grit into his nostrils. Jack found a tiny creek and led Kata over to plunge his muzzle gratefully into the cooling water. The wolf dog lapped happily, letting the water run over his tongue.

"Better not take too long, Jack," the constable said. "We're getting into the foothills now, and Black-Crow says he can see signs of Bart's passing this way."

The Indian had noted a pebble dislodged here and there, or a branch broken where the man ahead had pushed it aside. To his practiced eye these signs were as clear as a printed map.

"We are catching up with him," Black-Crow said. "Let us hope that he does not know it yet."

"You're right," said McTavish. "We don't want him lying in wait for us somewhere, in an ambush."

"I think Kata could tell if he does, sir," Jack said. "He's got his nose to the ground on the trail, but he's watching ahead, too." The wolf dog pricked up his ears at the sound of Jack's voice, and came over to put his head against the boy's knee.

"He really loves you, doesn't he?" said the constable. "I guess you're right. I wouldn't want to be Bart and try to tangle with that wolf while you're anywhere around."

Jack rumpled the wolf dog's ears, and then stood up. "Come on, Kata, time to start on." He didn't want to show his feelings in front of the constable, but inside he was wildly elated. Kata was showing his stuff! He was showing that he really could track, and moreover, that he was a steady worker. The wolf dog hadn't paid the slightest attention to the numerous game trails they crossed. Even the occasional small animals, slipping like shadows back into the trees as the men passed, did not deter him.

As dusk drew near, it was clear from Kata's increasing excitement that the trail was getting warmer. The constable suggested they continue to go as fast as possible, but that he and Black-Crow should keep their rifles ready, and constantly watch the territory ahead. "No telling whether Bart knows we're after him by now, and I'm not taking any chances of our getting caught unawares."

But they made camp that night without any signs of danger. Only Kata seemed restless, and whined as Jack tied him up for the night.

"I think we'd be smart to keep a watch tonight," the constable said. "I'll take the first half, and you can take the rest, Black-Crow. Jack, you'd better sleep; you need all the rest you can get for the hard part tomorrow, and Kata too."

The boy rolled up in his blankets and had no trouble following the constable's instructions, as he was very tired. Kata curled up close to him with his head on his paws, but the wolf dog did not sleep. He lay with his eyes open, steadily watching the black fastnesses of the forest beyond the flickering firelight. He knew that the man they were following was now very close, and he sensed that this man would do harm to his master. The big wolf dog, tired though he was, could not rest.

At midnight McTavish woke Black-Crow. They held a whispered consultation to keep from waking Jack. "I think," said the Indian, "that this Bart is very close by. Before you sleep I will go into the forest ahead, to see what I can find. We must take no chances now, and the dog seems uneasy. See, he does not sleep."

"All right," agreed McTavish. "I'll keep watch here while you take a look ahead. It's so dark I can't see much outside of the firelight, and you move much quieter in the woods than I could. Don't be too long about it, though."

The Indian vanished in the darkness, and for a half-hour McTavish waited in silence. Then, as suddenly as he had gone, Black-Crow appeared again at the fireside. "I have found him," he said. "The dog is right. Bart sleeps about two miles from here, with his rifle beside him. His fire is almost out, and soon the cold will wake him. When he gets up to replenish it, he may see the smoke from our fire."

"Right you are. We'd better put it out."

Then the Indian woke Jack. "The man is ahead," he said. "You must keep Kata from barking. From now on we must stalk as carefully as the fox, in complete silence."

Jack nodded, and held tightly to Kata's leash. "What's your plan?" he asked McTavish.

"We'll wait till daybreak," the constable said, "and then we'll sneak up within a quarter-mile of Bart's camp. After that, if he's still there, Black-Crow and I'll go in after him."

"What if he's gone on?" Jack asked.

"Then we'll follow him. Black-Crow says he's camped at the mouth of a narrow ravine, so he can only go one way now. We'll go on ahead of you and

Kata, on either side of the ravine, and close in when Bart stops to rest."

Before dawn they rolled up their blankets, and in the pitch-darkness the Indian took the lead. Stepping exactly where Black-Crow did, Jack and the constable made no sound, for the Indian knew how to walk so no twig would crack underfoot, breaking the stillness of the forest. For some distance he led the way, and then he stopped. "The camp is within a quarter-mile of here, due north."

"All right," said McTavish. "You and Kata wait here, Jack, while we go take a look. If he's gone on we'll come back for you, and if he's there, we'll take him by surprise. In either case, until you hear something, stay right where you are. And keep Kata quiet."

Jack sat down on a log to wait, and petted Kata. The big wolf dog was very tired, but his great heart was as willing as ever. He gave one or two tugs on the leash, trying to pull Jack after the men in the direction they had disappeared. "You've done your part, Kata," the boy said. "Just take it easy, fellow. They'll be back in a minute with Bart, and it's all because of you! If it weren't for you, they'd never have found him." The boy buried his face in Kata's ruff, and the wolf dog licked his hand.

After some time had passed, just as Jack was beginning to wonder what was taking Black-Crow and the constable so long, two rifle shots cracked on the still morning air. In the silence that followed, Kata leaped forward, the great muscles of his hindquarters bulging as he strained against the leash.

"Quiet, boy. We've got to wait here, no matter what happens."

In a few minutes Black-Crow appeared from the woods, supporting the constable. "The convict saw him one moment too soon," the Indian said. "Now he has fled up the ravine. I would have followed, but I could not leave McTavish, and you."

"It's only a flesh wound in my arm," the constable said. "You go on. Take the wolf, and leave me here with Jack. You can come back for us later. We can't let Bart get away now!"

He grimaced with pain as the blood began to seep through his jacket sleeve, and Jack helped the Indian rip some of the cloth to make a bandage.

Then Black-Crow took Kata's leash. "Come with me, Wise One," he said, but Kata did not move. The Indian pulled him, but still Kata stood by Jack's side.

"I guess he won't leave me, Black-Crow," the boy said. "If it's okay to leave the constable here alone, I'll come with you."

"Of course," said McTavish. "Go ahead, but be careful. I'll be all right; just get that man!"

Jack and Black-Crow fixed the constable as com-

fortably as they could, and hurried on to the campsite. There Kata picked up the red-hot trail, which
led, as the Indian had predicted, into the ravine.

"We must be very careful now," Black-Crow said,
"for he knows we are after him, and there is no
way to judge what he will do."

They crept along the rocky stream bed in the
bottom of the ravine. Kata led them forward at a
rapid pace, straining at the leash.

Ahead, a rocky outcropping protruded from the
canyon wall, and as Black-Crow inched slowly
around it to look ahead, a shot rang out from the
opposite side of the ravine. The Indian jumped
backward, and Jack could hear the "ping" of the
bullet as it bounced off the rocks near his head!

The boy crept forward until he could crouch behind a boulder. Black-Crow signaled him on, and
Jack was almost even with the Indian when the rock
he was standing on slid sideways in the mud, and
Jack's foot slipped. With a gasp he stumbled and
fell, face downward, sprawled among the stones.

The leash slipped from Jack's hand as he fell, and
Kata leaped forward. His hackles rose, and his lips
wrinkled back in a terrible snarl while he tested the
wind with his nose. Then with a deep bark he
bounded across the stream bed toward the hidden
Bart, scrambled up the other side, and disappeared
behind the rocks of the opposite ledge.

Chapter 11

KATA'S DECISION

JACK SCRAMBLED to his feet in time to see Kata vanish into the boulders on the other side of the ravine.

"Keep back!" called Black-Crow warningly, as Jack started to follow. "Bart has his sights on us! We must not cross the ravine yet!"

"But what about Kata!" Jack said. "He'll get hurt!"

"The wolf dog can take care of himself, don't worry. Come, we must find a place to cross under cover."

166

They made their way back down the canyon, keeping well out of sight of the opposite side. Fifty yards away was a heavy growth of tamarack bushes growing across the dry stream bed. As they reached it they heard Kata's furious barking, echoing and re-echoing across the ravine. It came from beyond the ridge, and Jack jumped to his feet.

"Come on, Black-Crow, Kata's in trouble! Hurry, please!" Without waiting for the Indian's reply, the boy was off through the bushes. He ran across the rocks, clawing his way up the steep shale of the far side. Breathlessly he scrambled up the last few steps to the top. There he came to an abrupt halt. Not fifty feet away stood Kata, growling over the out-stretched figure of a man!

"Kata!" Jack shouted. "You've got him! Good boy, stay there while I go get Black-Crow!" The boy jumped back on the ledge and waved to the Indian. "Here he is, Black-Crow, and he's got Bart!"

The Indian strode over to the prone man and said, "Are you hurt?"

"No," growled the convict, "but get this cursed wolf devil away! I think he will kill me!"

"Yes, he will kill you, if you move." The Indian walked over and picked up the half-breed's rifle, lying where he had dropped it when Kata caught him by surprise.

"All right, Jack. Call Kata, and we'll let this scum of the city get up."

"I'd like to tell Kata to rip his throat out," Jack said, and Bart moaned with terror. "But I guess the constable's posse had better take care of him. Kata," his tone changed to the familiar command. "Come! Come, Kata!"

The wolf dog uttered an ugly snarl at the now petrified Bart, and slowly backed away, every hair on his back bristling. His fury rumbled in his throat, but he held true to his training, and made no further move toward the man.

"Now, get up!" Black-Crow said to Bart. "We have many miles to go."

Two weeks later the first snow came. It began early in the night, and by morning, when Jack got up to go to school, the ground was completely covered with white.

"Looks like we're in for an early winter," said Mr. Miller at breakfast. "Means a long steady snowfall when it starts quietly like this."

Jack looked up from the table to watch the deepening blanket outside. Kata sat by Jack's chair, and he too seemed to feel the difference in the air. He whined several times.

The big wolf dog spent most of his time in the

house now. While Jack was at school he usually stayed in the kitchen with Mrs. Miller, following her around, as she called it, "like a big pony." She had completely changed her mind about Kata after Bart's capture. The constable had told everyone that they never could have caught Bart without the wolf dog, and he was lavish in his praise of Jack's training as well.

"What I liked best," McTavish told Mrs. Miller, "was that Kata didn't try to hurt Bart. He just knocked him down and stood guard till Jack and Black-Crow could get there. Shows he really knows his stuff. I thought he was vicious, but that proved he isn't."

To Kata, catching Bart had been nothing more than a job Jack had given him. He had obeyed, as he would obey any order from his master. As for Bart, the wolf dog had felt no real desire to hurt him, once the danger to Jack was over.

"Well," Mrs. Miller had said, "I know we can trust him now. Your idea was right, Jack, when he bit that workman in Frontenac City. I suppose he just thought the man was going to hurt you, and used the only defense he knew. That certainly isn't vicious." She laughed at the wolf dog. "Look at him now, playing with that pesky kitten."

The police from Frontenac City had met the posse in Troutville, and taken the now cringing Bart away with them, but not before the commissioner, himself, had asked to see Jack. "I want to tell you, my boy, that without you and your wolf dog we would have lost our prisoner. You did a good job."

Jack felt a thrill of pride at the commissioner's words. Kata had proved himself, on his last chance! He had shown everyone he was perfectly trustworthy, and obedient as well.

"Thank you, sir," the boy said. "But Kata did it all. I only followed him, and if it hadn't been for his running across the ravine like that, we would never have caught up with Bart."

"Well, you did a fine job of training him, I'm certain of that. Wish we had some more like him to work with our police force."

"Any time you need him, sir, just call on the two of us," Jack said proudly. "Kata can follow any trail."

"I'll do that, my boy," the commissioner smiled. "And I won't forget what you and your wolf dog have done."

Since then there had been little going on in the settlement. Jack's school had started a week ago, and every day he left the house early in the morning, returning late in the afternoon. At first Kata tried frantically to follow, hurling himself against the door and whining for hours. No one could comfort him, for the wolf dog had become so accustomed to going everywhere with Jack he could not bear to be separated from him now. In a few days, however, he seemed to understand that Jack would return in the afternoon. After that he quieted down and made no effort to follow the boy. He still whined when Jack left the house, but the boy always gave him a friendly pat and said, "No, fellow, no," when the wolf dog tried to follow. "Stay here, Kata, stay here!"

Jack hated to leave Kata almost as much as the wolf dog hated being left, but there was still time for their daily romps. Often it was nearly dark when Jack got home, but he let Kata out of the house to race down to the barn, or romp wildly in the front yard until Mrs. Miller called the boy to supper. Kata no longer had to herd the cows, for they were kept penned all the time now. At the first sign of a threatening sky Mr. Miller had brought them into the milksheds. Each day he expected the blizzard, but though the sky was gray and leaden, the wind and snow did not come.

This morning there was still no wind, only the big fluffy flakes that fell as silently as feathers on the frozen ground outside.

"I don't like it," Luke said. "This snow'll go on for days, and pile up deep. Does, when there's no wind to drift it. Then when the blizzard comes on top of it, we'll really have some trouble."

"Oh, dear," said Mrs. Miller. "I hate to see us

snowed in so early. It's hard on Jack to break the trail to Troutville, when he goes to school."

"Oh, Mom, I'm all right," Jack said. "I've got my snowshoes, and I know how to use them. Just takes a little longer, that's all. Besides, this snow might not last, anyway."

"I think you're wrong there, son," his father said.

Mr. Miller's judgment proved right, for the snow fell silently for two more days and nights. When finally the sun broke through to shine brightly over a glittering landscape, the snow was well over three feet deep. That morning Jack used his snowshoes to get to school, and even then he floundered in the powdery snow at every step. By afternoon the temperature began to drop.

"We'll have a heavy frost tonight," Mr. Miller said. "That will make things easier tomorrow, when the crust is frozen, and we can walk on the surface."

After supper, Jack went into the kitchen to do his homework. Suzy was in bed, and his mother and father were reading in the living room. Kata lay on a rug near the kitchen stove, dozing in the warmth. Outside, the frost settled down across the countryside, and as the temperature went down the still air almost crackled from the cold.

Suddenly, Kata lifted his head. He listened, his ears up.

"What is it, fellow?" Jack said. "Want to go out?" He went to the door and held it open, but Kata only stood in the doorway and sniffed the air. "Brrr," Jack shivered. "It's too cold to leave the door open, Kata. Come back in."

The wolf dog lay down on the rug again with a thump, but this time he did not doze. Instead he rested his head on his paws, his great dark eyes staring unseeingly ahead.

"What's wrong with you, Kata?" Jack asked, stooping to rumple the wolf dog's ears. Kata whined a little, and Jack sat down at the kitchen table to finish his homework. The boy thought the wolf dog seemed uneasy, but he could not know that Kata's keen ears had heard, far in the distance, a wild and sinister cry. Drifting down the still night air, the wailing sound was one Kata had never heard before, but it seemed as familiar to the wolf dog as the sound of Jack's voice. When he lay down, the sound came again, disturbing him in a way he did not understand. He raised his head, listening to the chorus that echoed far beyond the fir forests, and the hackles rose on his neck.

Jack went into the living room. "Dad," he said, "I think there's something outside. Kata keeps whining."

"I'll go and see," said Mr. Miller, rising to get his flashlight. "Might be another cougar, though it's a little early yet. Call Kata." They went out on the front porch, but there was no sign of any disturbance. Kata walked out on the lawn and sniffed the air, but the wailing cry had ceased, fading into the night.

"I'll just go down to the barn and make sure everything is all right," Mr. Miller said. "You go on inside, Jack, and finish your homework."

When he came back to the house Mr. Miller reported that all was quiet around the barns and the chicken houses. "Kata must have had a bad dream," he said. "He seems perfectly quiet now."

"Guess so, Dad, but I know something was bothering him."

Several days later Jack got home early from school and took Kata for a long hike across the back pastures. "Maybe if you get some hard exercise you won't get restless again," Jack told the wolf dog.

Beyond the pastures the fir trees stood silent and black in the white snow. Jack whistled to Kata as he climbed the fence. "We've got plenty of time today, fellow, let's go look for rabbit tracks. Ought to be easy enough to find in this snow." Jack had left his snowshoes at the house, and he and Kata floundered in the soft snow under the trees. The woods were very still, as though the heavy snowfall had muffled every living thing. Gone was the teeming woodland of the summer, and instead the woods

seemed silent and empty. "It's like being in ghost-
land," Jack whispered to Kata, and his voice echoed
in the distance. The great northern winter had de-
scended upon the frozen land and few animals were
abroad in this pitiless cold.

Jack kept on, feeling like an explorer in a changed
landscape, but soon he noticed that the sun was
dropping on the horizon.

"Come, Kata, we'd better go back. It's getting
late," he said, but he saw that Kata had stopped, and
was growling. "What is it, boy?" The wolf dog was
standing by a little frozen brook, and as Jack's eyes
followed him, the boy's glance was caught by a red
stain in the snow. He ran forward and then stopped
short at the edge of the brook. Kata was sniffing
carefully at the remains of a freshly killed buck, and
all around it were big tracks in the snow!

Quickly Jack bent down to examine them more
closely. "Why, Kata," he exclaimed, "they look like
your footprints!" Then the truth dawned on him.
They couldn't be Kata's tracks! The wolf dog had
been right with Jack all afternoon, and he would
never roam this far alone. "They must be . . . they
must be wolf tracks!" Jack said. He got to his feet
and peered around in the fading light. Now the trees
were blending into the dusk, no longer sharply out-
lined. The long forest aisles were filled with the mists
of twilight, and suddenly the fir forest seemed wild

and mysterious, and somehow forbidding. A shiver ran up Jack's spine. The wolves! This close to the farm!

"Come on, Kata, let's go," he said. The wolf dog was growling into the gloom, but his growl ended in a whine. He sensed that the wolves were out there somewhere. Strange forces were working in his brain, and he felt a desire to go to meet the pack. Somehow he wanted to go not as an enemy, but as a friend. He scarcely heard Jack call him until the boy said again, "Come, Kata." Then the wolf dog reluctantly walked to his waiting master. "Good boy," Jack said. "We've got to hurry before it gets dark."

They hurried back through the deepening dusk. In his eagerness to explore the snowy woods, Jack had come farther than he thought, and it took some time to reach the pasture fence. When they came into the milkshed yard, Jack breathed a sigh of relief. "I'm pretty sure those wolves are far away by now, but I didn't like the idea of being out there after dark. You don't like it either, do you, Kata?" The wolf dog turned and looked back across the pasture at the fir trees, dimly silhouetted now against the last of the daylight. Again he growled, and then turned to follow Jack up to the farmhouse.

That night, Jack was worried, for Kata was still restless and uneasy. He had said nothing to his parents about the wolf tracks. Jack knew he would have to settle this alone. Suppose they had been right? Suppose, now that Kata was grown, and winter had come, he really had grown into a wolf, instead of a dog? Jack knew the wolf dog's uneasiness came mostly from his divided instincts, and somehow he must give Kata the chance to choose. Jack knew, too, his father would tell him to keep Kata shut up in the house until the wolves had left the vicinity of the farm. But Jack could not do that. If Kata was to be his dog, Kata must, as Black-Crow had said long ago, stay because of love, not be held by force.

Resolutely Jack turned back to his homework. There was nothing he could do now, anyway. The quiet of the kitchen was broken only by his scratching pen and the ticking clock. Once, Jack glanced at Kata, dozing peacefully in front of the stove, and for a minute he wondered if he had imagined the slain buck and the wolf tracks. But no, he knew they were real. The wolves were out there, somewhere, and all he could do was wait. An hour passed, and Jack was nearly finished. Then, soundlessly, Kata raised his head. He seemed to be listening, though Jack could hear nothing. The wolf dog got up and padded over to the window by the kitchen table, where he stood looking out, his breath clouding the frosty windowpane.

Jack started to speak, but then he held silent. This must be Kata's choice and the boy would do nothing to influence him. When Kata turned, Jack saw the bewilderment in the wolf dog's eyes, and he longed to reach out and rumple Kata's ears in the old affectionate way. But that would not be playing square, and he only watched as the wolf dog began to circle the room. Once, twice, he walked around, halting only to listen to the faint wailing chorus of the wolf pack, too distant for any human ears to hear. Then he went to the door, and whined. Quickly Jack pulled on his jacket and opened the door, and Kata bounded down the back steps.

The moon had risen, flooding the snowy yard with an eerie light that shimmered on Kata's jet-black coat. The intense cold made Jack shiver, but he waited in the doorway, watching Kata. The wolf dog stood perfectly still in the middle of the yard, like some huge creature the boy had never seen before. His eyes glowed red, and Jack shook his head, blinking. If he had not known it was Kata, he would have thought a wolf was standing there, lips drawn back in a silent snarl.

Then Kata stiffened, and now Jack heard it, too. Echoing on the still night air, the black forests and the glittering white pastures came the beckoning cry.

Still Kata did not move. His eyes were riveted on the distant fir trees as though he were straining to see into the blackness. In the doorway behind him was the master he worshiped. Ahead, in the forest, lay . . . what? Kata trembled as the howl echoed again—a furious cry now as the pack caught the scent of prey. The howls of the bloodthirsty and starving wolves came like banshees to the wolf dog.

Suddenly Kata shuddered, and something snapped in his brain. His bewilderment was gone. At last his instincts, grown now, told him what distant trail the pack would follow, what luckless prey they would bring down, to feast on for hours under the moonlit sky. As plainly as if he could see the pack, Kata knew. Now they were closing in, now the great gray leader would leap forward, holding the moose at bay. Now the shifting, leaping shadows would emerge from the forest gloom, snarling, skulking, on every side of the doomed animal. Bellowing, the moose would charge, and a wolf leap forward for the hamstring. Now the leader would slash in, ripping the jugular, and the moose would sink into the snow, his crimson life-blood spurting on his chest.

Now the pack would gorge on red meat, and sleep until tomorrow. Tomorrow, when they would prowl, eyes glittering again with hunger, in search of further prey. Then, Kata knew, they might come closer. Here, to the farm! And his master was here! The master he must always obey and protect with all the strength he had, with a cunning that must match the wolf pack!

Again the howl echoed across the silent farmland,

the howl of the kill! As he had done in the forest glade when he fought the weasel, and in the house in Frontenac City, Kata threw back his great head and answered the call. But this time, tearing out of his throat into the frosty air, came an angry roar of defiance, hurled to the pack that might harm his master.

Silence fell again upon the yard, and Kata turned his head and looked at Jack. The boy did not speak, but he could see the wolf dog's eyes. No longer were they the eyes of a bewildered puppy, or the gleaming eyes of a great wolf, red with blood. Now, strong and sure, they shone with love, and the boy knew that Kata had made his own decision.

"Kata," he called softly, and the wolf dog came quickly across the snow. "Oh, Kata," Jack said again, when the wolf dog licked his hand. "Come on, fellow, it's cold out here. We'd better go inside and get warm!"

Then he opened the door, and Kata trotted eagerly into the kitchen. Jack sat down again at the table, and the great wolf dog walked over to rest his head for a moment on the boy's knee. With a contented sigh, he curled up on the rug at Jack's feet. He would rest now, for tomorrow he must be ready to protect the farm.